The Colors of Memory

The Colors of Memory

A Novel

Gabriela Tagliavini

HERODIAS

NEW YORK LONDON

Published by HERODIAS, INC.
346 First Avenue, New York, NY 10009
HERODIAS, LTD.
24 Lacy Road, London, SW15 1NL
www.herodias.com

Manufactured in the United States of America

Design by Stephanie Frey

Library of Congress Cataloging-in-Publication Data

Tagliavini, Gabriela, 1968-
[Colores de la memoria. English.]
The colors of memory : a novel / Gabriela Tagliavini. –1st ed.
p. cm.
ISBN 1-928746-17-9 (hb)
I. Title.
PQ7798.3.A45 C6513 2000
863'.64 — dc21
00-044891

British Library Cataloguing in Publication Data

A catalogue record of this book is available from the British Library.

Originally published as *Los Colores de la Memoria*
ISBN: 950-724-861-7
Lumen, Buenos Aires

ISBN 1-928746-17-9

1 3 5 7 9 8 6 4 2

First edition 2001

To the memory of
my father,
my always present muse
with mustache

To Jose,
my best friend and
my worst enemy

To my mother and brother,
for the inspiring traumas,
the night tales,
and the embracing laughs

. . . immobile nostalgias in an autumn well,

feelings unbearably present

which refuse to die there in the darkness.

The forgetfulness is so filled with memories

that sometimes events we re-remember don't fit in

so we have to throw away rancors. . . .

—Mario Benedetti

The Colors of Memory

Orange

I hate the morning rays that bounce on the window-panes, casting an orange shadow over my sheets, over my bones filled with bad memories. I hate the color orange for no apparent reason. In this place, they force me to drink orange juice. Kids love orange juice. I hate kids, babies. I never wanted to have one inside me. No one gets inside me. I'm not lying.

I hate this country; I hate Mexico. But I can't go back to the States because Americans hate me. So do you. And if you don't hate me yet, you will learn to hate me.

Outside my room, a family is crying. I hate groups, societies, fraternities, families, people who need others.

I hate this place, the noises of this place. The noise of high heels clopping down long corridors, the footsteps of the sick guy upstairs, the tick tock-tick tock of the wall clock, people blabbing in closed rooms, the constant buzzing of the air conditioning. I hate summer because no one gets depressed. In summer everything is too bright, everything is exposed.

Generally, I like hospitals. I like the cold decor always in light, pale blue or blind-eye white. The smells of ammonia, warm milk, disinfectant, Clorox: they cover up the smell of blood. Also, I like the long, interminable corridors, the gleaming tiles and the feeling that behind any one of those closed, white doors someone could be dying.

Strangely, I like the color white; it has all the colors inside; yet, not everyone can see them because they are hiding.

During the day, I don't do much. Right now, I'm adding zeros to my medical chart and clicking through TV channels. I push the French-vanilla alarm button so I can see the nurses' faces, purple like plums, when they come running in.

A short, ugly, raisin-faced woman doctor rushes in and says, "Not again ...!"

I smile cynically as I turn to the window. What I like to do the most is look out the window and count colors. I count the colors I see, then add them up to know which color wins. One tile red Impala convertible, a kid in a red soccer T-shirt: that makes two reds. Three reds, counting the neon sign over a bar that sells tacos. Counting colors makes me feel calm. Of course, I never count orange.

The woman doctor gives me some pills that make me less intelligent; so I have developed the ability to push them softly with my tongue and spit them to the floor. Even though she frowns, I know she likes to pick them up.

Every day I wake up at five, when the sable night starts to leave me and I take two palliatives and a glass of water with sugar. The doctors don't give me the brand of painkillers I want; they give me other brands I don't trust. So I hide my own pills and sugar packets under my pillow just in case my chest hurts. It's good to kill pain before it arrives.

At dawn when I awoke, I saw gloomy forms in front of the fading red from a neon light at a taco stand. An hour after I opened my eyes, the familiar banging on the wall and the yells, asking me to lower the volume. The main reason I wake up at 5 A.M. is to bother the other patients by putting the TV volume up really high. On Channel 24 a new couple in another part of the world gets married every morning at 6 A.M. TV has taught me how to make low-fat tiramisu and how to use a gun.

The doctor tells me, "Stop pushing the alarm button for no reason. I have to talk to you about the progress of your leukemia, Mrs. Carla . . ."

I don't like it when she calls me Mrs. Carla; I would prefer she call me Carla Arnone; I don't feel quite complete without my last name. Besides, I'm not a "Mrs.," I'm a "Miss," and she should know that. Anyway, I don't believe the doctors when they say I'm going to die soon. Doctors are liars. I don't feel bad about death—on the contrary. I've been working on dying for several years now. I'm almost seventy, quit writing at forty, and stopped speaking two years ago. Death is taking her time.

I stopped speaking because I started hating the sound of my screeching old voice. I began to talk less and less, and one day I just stopped. Maybe I didn't have anything to say; I didn't really have anyone to talk to, either. It doesn't bother me. Besides, I don't need another person to think, and I don't need to talk about what really happened.

I hate people who talk too much, especially those who call themselves artists; no one becomes an artist until they die and people see what art they've really made of their lives.

A long time ago, I wanted to make art. I don't think I still do. I only wrote one thing, but I never finished it for external reasons. I don't even remember where I put the papers. Sometimes I don't remember things. Only sometimes.

The door opens and a gurney is pushed next to my bed.

3

As always, I pretend I don't care and cover my face with the sheets, peeping through them because they are almost transparent from so much use. The patient's face is covered with bloody, yellowing bandages, but I know he's very young from the size of his body. I can't stand kids. From here, I can see his grimy, black hair pushing up through the gauze and his charcoal gray nails grasping the white sheets. Before the kid, there was a stinky prisoner and, before that, an unshaven policeman. Why do I have to share my room? Just because rural hospitals get overcrowded? The short, raisin-faced doctor never answers my questions because I'm not talking.

She stands at the end of my bed, blathering: ". . . and since the cancer hit the bones, we've stopped your chemo treatment, so you may experience an increase of physical energy. Summing up, Mrs. Carla, I'm sorry . . . but you only have a week to live, at most."

I smile broadly. She looks at me, confused.

"Do you want me to contact anyone for you?"

As I turn to the wall that protects me, she leaves. Women doctors lie as much as men doctors. What do they know? I could die sooner; I hope it's sooner. One more Monday, or only a Sunday. I like deadlines. I like the freedom that knowing your dying date gives you. I have a week to change things . . . to change one thing.

I want to take bitterness out of memory, doing all the mean things I didn't do. One mean thing.

From here, I can see my car. I drove myself here a month ago and introduced myself with a short note asking for palliatives, just in case. They have constrained me to my bed, but I can leave whenever I want. They can't force me to stay, although I don't remember where I put my car keys. Sometimes I can't remember things. My brain probably has wrinkles all over it, like my forehead—curved lines like inverted smiles. I have them all around my tired eyes and on my skinny, sand-colored body. My thoughts may sound more energetic than other people my age, but that's because inside I have a bitter emptiness, a growing emptiness that has more strength than any happiness.

Search for colors. A light blue liquid constantly drips into my vein. My violet vein is popping out through my thin skin, turning a dark blue. Two blues.

I trust "Leukemia"; at least she is doing her job. My blood is stuck, but since they stopped the chemo, I can walk to the bathroom and everything. They say my death will be sudden; they say one day I just won't wake up. Meanwhile, I'm helping death by starving myself. I haven't eaten in three days. They call it nervous anemia. I call it "If I don't want to eat, I won't eat, goddamn it." To hell with them. My car is indigo blue and has beige seats.

Even though I'm on the fifth floor, I would like to be on the fourth to see more. Through the window, I'm watching the hospital parking lot and the unfriendly people rounding the corner behind it. A Mexican guy in fluorescent clothes, a hip teenager in a cherry red shirt and a prostitute in a cheap, silver dress all wait for the green light. One green, one silver, one fluorescent fuchsia . . . damn! I can't count. In my time, we all dressed in brown, pastel, or cream colors. As I watch them go by, I want to tell them to wear normal colors, but I just shut up. I don't know if I remember how to speak. My lips tighten, my jaw clenches hard, and I spit through the window. Yet, I don't observe the saliva fall. Instead, I wait a few seconds, and then I peek through the window. No change. From here people seem very small, so I imagine they're under my control. I examine a group of them scurrying to cross the street. Where the hell are they going? What would happen if I threw something through the window, like a vase or one of these bags of blood?

In the hospital, everything is a potential weapon. Spoons can make eye catapults, books can crush skulls, and sheets can make perfect nooses.

An orange ant crawls up the wall, so I pick it up and toss it into my hot soup. I smile as I watch it struggle and spin around until it dies. With my fingers I twirl around a plastic fork and glare at my unsalted, egg-yellow noodle soup. Then I lift my head toward the window and focus on a businessman dressed in a burgundy suit walking up the street in my direction. I flip the plate out the window, then watch the liquid falling fast. The yellow and green soup coats the burgundy suit like an ugly watercolor. Some lady's makeup is also ruined, her salmon dress and red hair sticky with noodles. They swear at the window, but I hide my face. Morons. I hate people. I wish they were different. I wish they weren't afraid. I wish they were more like me.

I count the violet veins in my hands. Four, five, six, six and a half violets. Here in the hospital, you can smell death. People do all kinds of things out of fear of death. Some pa-

tients make ridiculous promises to God; others sew themselves to their days with hospital threads, not realizing we
die as we walk, as we sit as we sleep—we lose layers, dimen-
sions. I'm not afraid of death. Not anymore. Now I can do
whatever I want . . . the one thing I want.

The idea of killing someone crosses everybody's mind.
Some people stop this idea when they are children, some
after that; a few hold on to the idea forever. And when I say
forever, I mean like something that grows within you, like a
kidney or a rib.

Stretching the sheet, I make a knot, a hanging knot. I
haven't killed anyone yet, although I think about it constantly.

"Why did he have to die, God?! *Mi Dios ¿Por qué?*"
comes loudly from the corridor.

Without hesitation, I get out of bed and limp outside my
room. Even though I haven't murdered anyone, whenever I
hear someone has died here in the hospital, I can't resist
going to examine them, to see if they died naturally or if
they were killed. They seem more prune blue if they have
been strangled. Slowly I limp down the corridor and approach a stretcher where a women kneels; she is crying like
an old pig. I need to find out if the body is really dead, because I don't trust anyone.

On the stretcher lies a dead man; his face is cream-colored
like the sheets that cover him. A nurse pushes me back to my
room.

I guess I trusted someone once. A man. Okay, he wasn't
just a man. At least not to me. He was a liar, a thief. Not a big

thief though; he stole stories. He wasn't a good liar either. He said his name was Dmitri, but I never knew if it was true. As the years passed, I realized the more you live, the more you hate. I hate thousands, probably millions, of things, but I hate him more than orange.

Polished Brown

Hey, you. Nurse. Don't give me that needle. I don't need blood work. Where the hell does it say that I need blood work? I don't understand *your* Spanish, but don't call me "*loca.*" You're not a real nurse. You're a phony. I know it, only I can't prove it. I'm sure you're giving me the wrong medicine, and you'll sell the good one to a fancy pharmacy. I don't care if Prozac is in vogue. Why can't I have my old-fashioned palliatives?

The kid is sleeping and his jaw is slack. Hey, kid, wake up under your bandages. I want to yell this out, but no one hears me because I'm not talking. Okay, okay, don't push me, nurse; I'll lie still. I'm not dying, and you can't kill me. You can't kill someone who's already dead. I was nineteen years old when I started to die.

The need to write was in my blood, thickening in my veins. The year was 1953, and we lived in a trendy house in Los Feliz. It had chestnut-colored wooden walls and furniture, light beige carpet, and a small charcoal brown fireplace. We weren't rich—my father couldn't keep a steady job in Hollywood. So Pa worked for the FBI, helping them with "certain people." What else could he do in Hollywood in the fifties? Either you were a Red or you were against them; you couldn't just "be."

Pa had a corroded face with thick cheek bones, and he smiled with just his upper teeth. Broad, brown suit; big, brown tie; polished, brown shoes; extra thin mustache; brown hair with Bryl Cream; wide blue eyes that hurt when they looked at you.

Anyway, I liked my house during the day. There were always uncles and cousins and friends of my father hanging around, and I loved to hear the old people chatting, people who admired Pa.

Back then I wanted to be respected like him. I thought that if I were respected, the fear I had would stop—that overwhelming sense of fear, especially late in the afternoons after people left. So I tried the best I could to make Pa admire me. I wore my usual: brown men's work shoes with shoelaces, a perfectly starched shirt, loose gray pants with suspenders—men's clothes. In those days, most women didn't wear pants. And I always hid my gaze with a sad look I achieved by brushing my eyebrows down; and I thought my ankles were too skinny and my lips too thick. To make him proud, I spent my teenage years making up stories, while other girls made fools of themselves over boys. Writing, I was safe from my fear and from everything else.

I taught myself Spanish, Northern Italian, and linguistics because I didn't want to learn them at school with other young people; and I started working like grown-ups do. Normal people were boring to me; therefore I had no friends. I read everything from mysteries to Dante, from Hemingway to the Russians novelists, to the *Encyclopedia Britannica.* I thought books would answer all my questions about how to become balanced and adjusted; but books didn't make things clearer to me, they just made ideas spin around in my head. I don't blame books for what I am; we become what we are destined to become, sooner or later, no matter what we read or do.

My neighbors called me "Noni," like a grandmother, and the truth is that even before I turned twenty, my eyes looked ancient, duller than the others. Actually I wanted to be old because I thought that to be old was to be happy. So I became an adult at an early age. I decided I had suffered enough, so I removed all my feelings. Writing made me feel things without consequences. Art is a complete removal from living: if you take all feeling from a memory, it becomes a story.

Pa would drink vodka and orange juice in front of the radio and tell me I was beautiful, even though I wasn't. He said so because he wanted me to keep his secret from my mother. Mother didn't know anything about Pa's business. I still keep this secret and many others inside me. She's dead, and still I carry many secrets.

That day, as he rocked in his chair, listening to his mini-Radiola, I poured him more vodka and sat down by his side. The radio announced that Stalin had died after twenty-nine years of rule, that the Rosenbergs had finally been executed for treason, setting an example for other spies, and that Einsenhower had won New York city. But Pa never listened to the news, he was just waiting for his favorite show, *Gunsmoke*, and writing names on a piece of paper.

"Did I tell you about yesterday's son-of-a-bitch? That damned professor didn't want to talk. I threatened to cancel his Fulbright scholarship, but the Red bastard just wouldn't give any names."

I turned around to leave, but he grabbed my arm and

pulled me close to him. He caressed my hand like only he could. "Come back. You're looking pretty these days. Almost a woman."

"You're just telling me that 'cuz you don't want Mom to know, but everyone in Hollywood already knows what you do for a living."

"I told you, I don't care how many people know, I don't want your mama to know. I don't want her to get upset."

"Why do you tell me then?"

"I have to tell somebody, don't I? Like the guys who tell their friends after dating a gal. If you don't tell, it's like it never happened."

He wrote down another name on the paper. Then he thought in silence for a while before he continued adding to his list. I looked at it intrigued. "Those people . . . they're all bad, right?"

He nodded. "We aren't killing anyone here, you know. We don't ban people's lives, we only ban people's choices."

Whenever he got ready to go to work, I would help him fix his shirt and tie, standing on a khaki wooden stool by his closet. While he dressed, we used to sing, "You are my sunshine, my only sunshine . . ." I knew that made him feel happy, and I wanted him to be the happiest dad in the world, whether he was bad or not.

Pa used to tell my mother we were going to church, but twice a week he left me in a café to play cards with his old friends, while he went to do his dirty job. I saw him laughing with his boss, but I never saw his boss's face, only his wide shoulders walking away. I never liked cards, so I used to sit behind the window watching people walk by. The clothing, the cars, the dogs, pale red, indigo blue, two red, one sienna brown. Sometimes my father took a long time.

My mother never knew. It wasn't my fault; it was hers. She kept on playing the violin. She never wanted to know, I guess.

I grew up with death. Almost every week, we went to a funeral for one of my father's FBI friends.

Even at nineteen, I thought my future would be short and tragic. I was waiting for death to come for me at any moment; I even had a suitcase ready. Sometimes I would rehearse my last words in the bathroom mirror, trying to remember all the people I had to thank.

At night, I liked to play at being dead. I was really good at it. I would lie still in bed, slow down my breathing, and focus my eyes on the colors of the objects in my room without really seeing.

I was convinced that Pa would kill me, just as I thought he killed all those men by giving their names away. So every night I cleaned my room, in case death came when I was sleeping.

Pa never did anything to me I didn't deserve, anything too bad, but I know he wanted to. Every time I was alone with him in the house, I was scared. The way he stood and stared at me made me shiver. I think he had fear, too. Fear of his own thoughts.

In spite of it all, from the outside my house looked like a happy home. And my father wasn't always bad. He even gave me his watch once. Everybody loved my father—he was the tallest and the biggest and the best. I think I loved him, too.

———

Hollywood was a tacky glamorous place in the early fifties, with awful red-and-green neon signs that never matched the women in their pale colors—pastels and champagne tones. Almost everything was gray or brown. Cars were fat; refrigerators, too. During World War II, Hollywood became a military camp. Studios became hotels and hospitals for Marines, and studio trucks were used to transport army troops and equipment. To my naive eyes of nineteen, it was a mysterious, rich place, a star's ghetto, the light of the West, where famous people's faces gleamed.

When I followed Pa into the studio, he was always surrounded by three men dressed in gray, and the guard always remembered his name when he greeted him.

One day, one of the men in gray suits tried to follow us in as usual, but was stopped by the guard.

"I'm sorry, Mr. Rubenstein. You can't come in."

"What are you talking about? I've been working here for fifteen years." He turned to my father, "What's he talking about, Robert?"

"I'm sorry, Peter. The studio thinks you don't have the same drive you used to."

"Drive? I stayed at work until 11 P.M. yesterday. Everyone saw me. I can stay until midnight if you want me to. I have kids, you know. I can't lose . . ."

Pa didn't even answer him and the man walked away

without saying a word. Rubenstein knew there was nothing he could say to keep his job. As he disappeared, Pa turned to the other two men and delivered a speech I would never forget.

"Why people in this country would sympathize with the Red culture is beyond my understanding. I suppose "subversive" is almost a synonym for "artist." Artists always like to test boundaries, to see when the rope is gonna break. But if you're a Commie, the rope always breaks."

I didn't understand what he was saying, but it sounded good to me, so I hugged him.

"Bye. Have a good day, darling," he said.

"Do you have to go now? What time is it, Pa?"

And that's when it happened. Pa glanced at his wrist and gave me his fancy chronograph watch. "You can borrow it for today."

The watch looked bigger on my wrist than on his. I leaned forward and whispered in his ear, "Are you giving it to me because you don't want me to tell Mom what you're working on?"

He lowered his eyes, suddenly vulnerable. I caressed his head. "Don't worry, Daddy. I won't tell her."

I kissed him lightly on the cheek, and he left, as always, in a direction opposite to mine—toward the movie section of the studio. Several groups of women walked in my direction, toward the television network. There weren't many women in movies, only makeup artists and script girls. My female coworkers wore pastel-colored dresses and always sneered at my masculine suit.

On the way into my office, I usually stopped by the studio's screening room. That day, a poster for *From Here to Eternity* was displayed. I had seen it eleven times.

I worked freelance for the studio's television network, writing commentaries for political reporters who had a Sunday morning program. Of course, I got the job "recommended" by Pa; I summarized political polls every day, while others did the more important writing. I hated my boss in his wide-brimmed hats. I hated that job. I hated politics, journalism. I hated nonfiction. I hated reality. My reality.

My boss, Mr. Markins, polished my grammar and never put my name in the credits. I guess the job was okay for a teenager like me, full of complaints, and also for a woman in 1953. I really wanted to quit to prove to all those reporters who wore round glasses that I was better than they were, and to all the people who knew Pa that I was as good as he was. But to do that I had to be a real writer. A real writer doesn't die.

I was typing fast at my Olivetti when Mr. Markins called to me. He never, ever took off his hat, and he smoked using a long Bristol cigarette holder. He pulled the sheet from my typewriter and put it aside without reading it. Then he gestured to five people to come gather around him, four men and me.

"Gentlemen, the network wants more shows reflecting the people's war against the Lefties. Not a word on the Communist conspiracy in Hollywood—we don't want to upset viewers. Only stories on Americanism, patriotism. More about the heroes who cooperated, that sort of thing. You,

Johnny, get an interview with Elia Kazan." Johnny the brown-noser nodded as the other writers scribbled in their notebooks. I didn't write a word; I just looked at Mr. Markins and paid close attention.

"You, Carla, my best man in the field, follow me. I got something for you."

He gestured for me to follow him and walked away from the group. I obeyed him, following him to a long empty corridor.

"Carla, I need you to cover the delegation from the House Un-American Activities Committee at San Pedro port for tonight's show."

"What for? Aren't they doing a good job?"

"Are you kidding me? They're doing an excellent job, cleaning up this country of all the pink filth. You'll see . . . in fifty years or so, the Russians will be working for us. I just need you to interview a couple of people down there saying the Committee is doing a good job. Just do it, will you?"

"If I run into people who are against the Committee, do I interview them too?"

"There aren't any people who are against the Committee. Look, I know you want to write something more—how can I say it—risky. But our show is not . . ."

"Did you read the pages I gave you?"

"Yeah."

"And?"

"You use too many adjectives. You analyze things too much. Your writing lacks maturity. Maybe if you and I . . ." As we neared the bathroom door, he checked that no one was around, and got closer, touching my hair. "Maybe if you changed your situation . . . freed your inhibitions. We could talk about this later over a very dry martini."

Angry, I grabbed my notebook and darted into the bathroom. I didn't agree with him; what did my sexuality have to do with my vision of life?

I pulled my jacket close around me and brushed my short hair back with Bryl Cream to be unattractive to men. It wasn't my goal to seduce anyone; I only cared about writing. But I needed a man for my screenplay, and the only way to find one was to be among them. To be among men, I believed I had to pretend I was one.

My friend Barbara said I looked beautiful with that style, but I wanted to look ugly. Barbara was my pal. She was a chubby woman who wore her hair up like Evita.

"Why would you want to look bad? That's crazy," she said.

"Told you, the only way to hang out with men is to look like one."

"Why would you . . . ? Are you still looking for a guy to write about? Is that it?" She laughed at me, she always did. "Why don't you stop with that screenplay crap? Only men write movies. Take a look around you. We women only write for television. Why don't you write about what's going on in the country? Didn't you hear? They blacklisted two more people here yesterday—write about that."

"So they'll subpoena me like they did you?"

"I'm out, aren't I? All it took was for me to say I was sorry. Why don't you write something political, something serious, instead of lying to yourself, making up stories?"

We faced each other in the mirror. As Barbara applied more make-up to her face, I washed mine off.

"One can take things from reality and turn them into fiction without lying. I think. One can observe reality and have an angle on it. I want my expertise to be people's lives."

"Whose life?" Barbara asked.

"I'm gonna find him."

"Who?"

"My character. The one I'm gonna make famous with a screenplay based on his life. Why am I even explaining this to you? I'm gonna borrow an interesting life and make it mine, do you get it? A character who doesn't fear death or water or anything, a character like . . . well, not like me."

Because I couldn't change my own past, I wanted to change other people's pasts with my writing. After they read about my character, they wouldn't be afraid of anything, not even death. I was erasing my own fears or maybe making them invisible, and I wanted to write the perfect screenplay that reflected that, so I was searching in bars for the perfect character. A character who would have no fear. I wanted to borrow a life more interesting and intriguing than mine; I found that life one winter evening in 1953.

Oceanic Blue

I can still remember some things, kid. I want to tell the kid who's next to me the whole story of my life, but instead, I keep it to myself. The kid is sketching things on paper. Whatever he is outlining, he is doing it from memory, because his eyes are still bandaged. From my bed, I can't see what he's drawing. I think it's a man's face, maybe his father, as if he could hear my thoughts. I try to peek, but I can't see the picture. He rolls over, and I glance at the sketch. The face in the drawing is a round circle and the eyes are two Xs. I wish I could see more, but I don't want to ask. The kid keeps drawing even though his eyes are closed. I don't care if he doesn't want to show me; he can't see me, either. I throw the orange juice in the bed pan.

For my screenplay, I kept a notebook describing places and everything that to me seemed unusual—how people moved their faces and why. I invented new names and lives for them and I took notes on the colors people wore. You can tell a lot about people by the colors they wear. For example: All the women who dress in black want to be skinnier. Most of the women who wear burgundy lipstick are from Brazil. The men who have pink bald heads generally have lots of stories to tell.

In those days, everything moved more slowly; people walked dragging their feet and had time to hang out for hours in bars. Time itself moved more slowly. Because I spoke so fast that I stuttered and walked so quickly that I tripped, I preferred to shut up and write. I invited every drunk man I met on the street to sit with me at the nearest bar and talk about his life. At nineteen, I wasn't allowed to drink, so I stayed sober and listened. After a couple of drinks, most people told their deepest secrets. I became an expert on other people's lives. But I had to find the one life story that was worth telling.

Usually I went to small conservative bars like the Brown Derby, Musso and Frank, or the Hollywood Guild and Canteen, where all the studio executives went. Somewhere on Hollywood Boulevard between La Brea and Highland. But not that night. I had finished my piece on the San Pedro port, so I walked and walked by the sea rocks and ended up in a shabby bar by the pier.

When I saw my reflection in the water beneath a lamppost, I stepped back, afraid I would fall in. Two guys were outside the bar, sitting on the round hood of a car. I nodded to them, and to avoid the one who came after me, I entered. The bar had no windows; it was like night inside all day. Rusty chains criss-crossed the mural walls like garlands, and fat barrels of beer spilt their contents into sailors' mouths. It was late, and I was drinking ginger ale and writing down behaviors and colors. In the bar there were weird people—bums asking for change, prostitutes with no teeth, drunk marines, drunk Mexicans, drunk Indians. A couple talked about Abbott & Costello. Some other couples danced the Jitterbug, swinging around and falling down from the alcohol. The music of Tommy and Jimmy Dorsey was so loud I could feel it bouncing off the walls.

I approached the bar, where a young bartender with a lighthouse tattoo leaned, and ordered another ginger ale. A drunk fisherman inched up to me. The veins in his eyes were yellow like his pants, his skin rough, his olive-colored mustache covered with beer foam.

"Matilda left me," he said. "I'm frightened as a fish who's already bit the bait."

While the fisherman kept talking, I changed seats. I had already heard the story of lost love. Besides, I couldn't stand it that he wore red socks with yellow pants. How could some people not pay attention to colors?

"I've told you a hundred times not to move, damn it," a drunk was telling the wall.

"Listen," I said, "I'll buy you a beer if you tell me about your life."

"I'll tell you for free. What do you want to know?"

"If you are afraid of anything."

"Many things, starting with my mother."

I moved on. Fumbling and looking around I noticed a circle of ten men laughing at the other end of the bar. In the middle of it, an almost-white-from-the-sun blond sailor was doing card tricks for the men. He was wearing a tight, white T-shirt and his arms moved like wings. I could see his muscular upper arm flex back and forth with a card in his fingers. His tall body looked twenty something, but the half-profile of his buoyant face looked much younger, like a kid's. I moved forward to see him better. He did his dodges and sleights of hand, and the people applauded, laughing. But he wasn't going to fool *me* with magic.

He flipped three cards and asked a fat man to pick the ace. He shuffled the cards so fast he lost me. I used to be good with cards, but he was faster. I'd catch him next time, I thought, and approached tentatively, peeking between their backs. I noticed the sailor's socks: perfectly white like his T-shirt.

He looked at me with a virile gaze, nodded as if he wanted to tell me something, and turned his face back to the men. I pretended to look around casually, then awkwardly walked backwards. The sailor stopped laughing, whispered something to his audience, left them, and approached me. He strode across the room appraisingly; the lamps illuminated him and then left him in shadows. As far as I was from him, I could see his unshaven light bronze skin and small nose, flat like a boxer's. He stared at me with curiosity. He had exotic dark blue eyes, onyx-blue. Or were they black? Black as melted asphalt. They seemed arrogant or maybe lonely, and he had a mole under his left eye.

I wrote his colors: café au lait *skin, oceanic blue eyes, tricky black mole.*

As he approached me, he smiled impudently. Everything was perfect until I focused on his insane grin. His front teeth were too small, separated, and the space between them ruined his smile. His smirk was slow, so slow he looked crazy. What always scared me about the idea of becoming crazy was not the illness itself, but the certainty that if you became crazy no one would understand you. He looked defiant, as if he didn't care what people thought about him, and kept gliding toward me. I primly raised my chest.

When he halted in front of me, I noticed he was much taller than I. I squinted up. His audacious eyes swept across me. He stared at my skinny body and my breasts, which were never much to look at.

We couldn't talk because the music was so loud. I tried to say hello, but my voice didn't come out. He took another step and stopped closer, standing in front of me, waiting for me to repeat what I had said. I didn't. I didn't know what to say. He was tall and big and good-looking. I gave him a shy smile. I lowered my head and glanced at his delicate and wise hands. His fingers were bony and long like a woman's, his nails polished like a rock made smooth by the water on the shore.

We were very close, standing morosely silent, staring into each other's eyes. At that close range, his daring gaze felt calm like snow.

Then he looked oddly at the floor, and I followed his vision to see if he had lost something. He glanced at me for a second in a curious way and then began to walk away, accidentally bumping my arm as he passed.

"Sorry," he mumbled and grabbed my wrist. I extended my fingers, wanting to hold his hand, but he slipped through my grasp.

"No . . ." I murmured.

He walked to the door and left the place without glancing back at me. I stood there for a while, frozen. Then I maniacally ran to the door, but he had vanished into a thick, violet fog; only the port lights broke the darkness. Abruptly I went back inside and angrily ordered another ginger ale from the young bartender with the lighthouse tattoo.

"Who was that blond guy?" I asked him while I paid.

"Why? You interested in him, eh?"

"The son of a bitch stole my watch." I showed the bartender my naked wrist.

"God! That guy! Not again."

"What do you mean? He does it all the time?"

"Hell, yeah. He's so dumb sometimes he steals lousy and cheap watches."

"What's his name?"

"Dmitri," the bartender said, cleaning a glass.

"Where does he sell the watches? I kind of want to get mine back."

"He doesn't sell them. Said he only wants one kind of watch."

"What kind?"

"I don't know."

I drank silently until the shy dawn peeked under the door. I remembered the scene over and over and pondered his eyes, because I couldn't remember if they were blue or black. He had a certainty about him, he wasn't afraid of getting caught, and he lived at the harbor, so he obviously wasn't afraid of water. Maybe he wasn't afraid of anything, not even death. And what a great taste for color. Too bad about the teeth. But I could forget them, because I knew right away that he was the character I wanted for my screenplay, a man who generated questions.

Skin Bronze

Well, kid, I thought Dmitri was going to be an experience you forget as quickly as you forget caprice. I thought I would kill the past, filling in the present with new unknown people—but the past breathes in the everyday present. I hope you can hear me under those bandages, kid.

The kid mutters something, but he's not talking to me. I haven't said anything.

The night after Dmitri stole my watch, I finished another piece about the Committee for the network and decided not to go back home. Instead I went down to the harbor bar were I had met him, waited outside until he came out at 6 P.M., and followed him to the port of Long Beach. To pass time, I was counting colors in the fading light, in the anxious, late-day atmosphere of the harbor. A rusty chain, apple boxes, wooden boxes, cardboard boxes, and grimy water. No doubt the harbor is a brown place. The color brown reminded me of Pa's tie. It reminded me of death.

I walked behind him, hiding in dark alleyways, closing doors like in the movies, and I even wore a long, dark coat. It started to rain; the water started to pelt my shoulders as hard as if the drops were jabbing fingers. Marines were running all over, carrying equipment into battleship gray vessels. Searchlights tunneled into the rain. The smell of nervous, sweating people and gunpowder filled the place, making the salty ocean air smell like danger. Danger one longs for.

I walked quietly, one cautious footstep after the other on

the wet streets. The rain crawled on the pavement, looking for a way out to the ocean. He walked jumping, almost dancing, waving his muscular arms. It seemed as if he actually enjoyed the rain.

I followed him to his boat and sat on a yellow garbage can, watching him from a place behind a storage drum ten feet away. It was an old fishing boat—tiny, and the sails were dirty. Nets hung on both sides, along with a couple of old tires, and a can of worms lay beside the wooden helm. He jumped to the deck and walked forward to arrange the sail. I could see him spinning the railing while he stood to one side of the mast. Then he sat on a small navy blue chair and leaned back on the ivory deck, letting the rain pour over him, like thin snow. His hair dripped water over his chest. He cleaned his fingernails with a pocket knife. Meanwhile he stretched his legs, slid his boots off, and his naked feet touched the sprit at the bow of the boat. He was drinking a dark beer and wearing worn out jeans. Because I wasn't sure about his eye color, I counted them as the second blue and the second black.

Later it started to rain harder, and he took off his T-shirt, grinning. I eyed him. His chest had almost no hair; his arms and shoulders were slender and wiry with muscles marked in little squares; his bronze skin was etched by the sea wind. He stayed like that, getting all wet. In the gleam of the water, his skin looked almost dark bronze—the only bronze color I could find.

Eventually the rain stopped. He took a toothbrush out of his pocket, dipped it into the sea water and put it in his mouth, cleaning his teeth and then bending down to clean the toothbrush in the harbor. There he stayed for almost two hours just staring at the quiet, magenta sky. I didn't see the point of staring at the sky; I couldn't see anything happening there. I noticed, however, that he wasn't just quiet, he was actually paying attention to the silence.

When the night arrived, everybody turned on their lights. Some people drew their curtains and the cars drove around with their fog lights on. While we both remained still, in the marina there was constant movement. I stayed staring at Dmitri for almost two more hours, his dark skin blending with the blackness of the night.

Just before nine o'clock, he began to talk to himself. I'm not sure if he was aware of it, maybe he believed he was just thinking. I couldn't hear what he was saying, so I guessed he was speaking to the sea. If not to the water, to whom? It didn't make any sense to speak only to oneself.

I wrote: *Ivory wooden boat, yellow lamps on deck, gray and magenta horizon.*

He watched the sky and my pen stopped. I wanted to write what he was thinking, or at least what I thought he was thinking, just sitting there in the same position. Not one word came to my mind. Just then I realized I didn't want to count colors.

A light from a distant boat gleamed, making the surface of the harbor shine, outlining his figure. His wrist shone. To my surprise, I noticed that he was wearing my watch.

I wondered why he was using it since he didn't seem to care about time. In fact, he hadn't even glanced at it in all the hours I had been watching him. Then I felt calm, knowing that Pa's was an underwater watch. Still, he must have so many watches; I wondered why he was wearing mine.

I left, walking through the brown, dirty harbor. Then I laughed, thinking I would change the scenery in my descriptions, invent another place for Dmitri's story. After all, I was the only one who knew the truth.

Sage Green

What do you mean, turning off my TV, nurse? What? I'm watching too much TV? If you don't turn on my TV again, I'm gonna sing. "Yesterday," that's my favorite song. And I'm gonna sing really loud, I swear. She doesn't glance at me because she doesn't hear me. I stare blankly through the window. Okay, nurse, I don't care, I can look down for a while. *Arrivederci,* asshole. You hear me? I know you can't hear me because I'm not talking, but if you wanted to you could listen. By observing, I listen even when people don't speak, just as I am a writer, even if I don't write any more.

She doesn't listen to me because she doesn't want to know me. No one knows me or will ever know me. I'm a chameleon; I hide behind colors. A long time ago I became my own mask.

Today they took the bandages off the face of the kid next to me. His face looks colorless, dull. He seems to be about ten years old, but he already has black circles under his watery, sage green eyes. Since morning, he's been punching holes in people's eyes in magazines. No one has come to visit him since he got here. He tried to communicate with me a couple of times, but I didn't answer. He points at a magazine ad, making one more attempt.

"Hi. What do you think of these sneakers?"

One empty, silver gray Jaguar; one cold, gray beam in the building across the street; two piles of dried pigeon shit: three, maybe four grays. I turn around; the kid is studying me. I don't know how long he has been watching me.

"What are you writing?" the kid asks.

I have to answer. I don't want to, but I have to. It would be really impolite if I didn't; after all, he is the first one to ask about me in years. It's not that I want to tell him my story. No one knows my story. I try to stop my answer, focusing on the colors of the pills on my bedside table. I don't want to answer. One red, two blues. I don't want to. I can't. One purple.

"What are you writing?"

Then I focus on the pills again—on the white line that divides the red coating. It's so thin, so fragile. I don't have to answer. I hear my answer climbing up my throat, making my lips move, leaving my mouth. "I'm . . . not writing," I mumble.

"I saw a notebook and a pen," he insists.

I grab the notebook from the table, showing him that it's blank.

"I carry it just in case," I remark, and smartly stare back out the window. "Besides, I'm not supposed to talk. I don't talk any more, you see?"

Looking down, I notice a flashy, turquoise bicycle outside on the street and add briefly, "Look, okay, kid. I was a writer in the past, but I'm not even sure if I was a good one."

That is a lie. I thought I was the best, even though everyone said I was too melodramatic. Writing is an act of faith that hurts; if you don't believe in your own phrases, you better quit. I also did that.

"Nobody can hurt me," the kid utters, as if he could hear my thoughts. "I'm ten years old, what do you think?," he scratches his little nose.

Why did I even talk to him? I have to get out of here.

"You know, I also want out. But I don't have anywhere to go."

I lift an eyebrow, pretending not to hear him. Didn't your mother tell you not to speak to strangers? I want to say, but I stay quiet.

"Mom got me here. Sometimes she scratches me." The kid moves his skinny fingers nervously when he talks. I notice an olive black pirate-sword earring in his right ear, and I wonder what it means, but I don't ask him.

"Mom works collecting cans at night and wakes up at four in the afternoon. But it's not my fault if she treats me like . . . I stole some money, that's all. To buy a Christmas . . . She said that Christmas was two months ago, she said no tree, and since it wasn't really hot yet, I thought we could have one now," he wipes mucus from his runny nose. "You know, when it's cold out, inside our apartment it's freezing, and in the summer it's an oven. I didn't think she'd catch me stealing in that market. I swear I tried to stay out of trouble. I just wanted a tree, not even a present. You think I did wrong?"

I don't even glance at him; I look through the window at the building on the corner. A wooden station wagon pulls up in front of a store, and the driver buys incense and candles. Through the window, I see that they sell crystals for healing, too. The streets are filled with people buying and selling awful, unnecessary things. I think the kid is lucky that his mother doesn't have money; otherwise he would be like those kids who buy a Nintendo game and then get epilepsy. Even though I don't look at the kid, I know he keeps watching me. I cross my arms over my chest like a corpse. I don't move at all. I'm not even here.

When the kid realizes I'm not going to talk, he continues. He mimics a slap: "Smash! And when I told her I didn't like the smell of her clothes drying on my futon, she got so mad that she scratched my face with those big red nails of hers. She said I'm like that jerk, my dad. But I doubt she remembers him at all. I don't."

The kid's pale sage green eyes glance at me to see my reaction. I don't give him any.

"Maybe I should try to find my dad. Tell him to buy a Christmas tree. The thing is, I don't have his picture."

I lie on my side facing the wall, my eyes pacing its paper pattern of light blue flowers. Although I don't look back at him, I feel his eyes on me.

"Okay. I know what I can do, it's easy. I have to search for a guy who looks just like me. He must be just like me. Mom doesn't have black hair. Dad must have. I know he speaks English . . . That's why she taught me English, in case he . . . What I need is someone who can come with me to that country above us and see if a man out there and me are alike." His eyes gleam, and he begins to yell. "Hey! I have an idea! Listen, lady! Ma' am! Hey! You. You can help me, Miss!"

I hate people who yell; kids always yell. Although I'm glad he calls me Miss and not Mrs.

"Hey! If you don't have anything to do . . . not that you don't, but if you don't . . . would you help me find my father?"

Of course, I make him ask twice before I answer. Maybe

three times.

"Would you?"

True, I promised not to talk to anyone until Dmitri talked to me first, but since the kid is right here I have to talk to him. Maybe I can talk again just this time; I suppose it counts as one time. "I wouldn't go with you from here to the corner," I hear the sound of my screechy voice. "Besides, I also have to look for somebody."

"For the watch thief?"

"How did you know, kid?"

" 'Cuz you been thinking out loud, Miss Carla. I listened to your whole story."

"Not all of it."

Paper White

Pa and I were about to leave home that morning, like always, singing, "You are my sunshine, my only sunshine . . ." when Mom stopped us by the door.

"You going out? But it's a holiday."

He kissed her briefly and said, "We're going to church."

Of course we weren't. Church was his cover-up for everything.

On the way to the House Un-American Activities Committee office, we stayed silent. Before we entered, he asked me, "You sure you want to see this?"

I nodded, looking at the daunting brick building. He caressed my hair as we entered, still murmuring, "You're my sunshine . . ."

It was an executive session. The room was smoggy, only a few rays of light came through the venetian blinds. A fat guy seated next to Pa chain-smoked in silence.

Behind them, there was a see-through two-way mirror. As I watched the room in awe protected by it, I wondered if my silhouette could be seen behind it.

At another desk in front of them, a Hollywood director was sweating, holding on to the table with his right hand. With the other hand, he waved a black and white picture of a woman. "You want me to accuse my wife?!"

Pa leaned back and said, "Well, she was a Communist, wasn't she? Or she still is?"

"I'm not gonna name my own fucking wife!"

Pa calmly rocked his chair. "Well, too damn bad because she named you."

I never heard a longer silence. It felt like in a movie, only it wasn't. It was real. The Hollywood director looked at the picture of his wife with disbelief. His hands shook, holding on to his beliefs. "She would never . . ."

"Women are so much more sensitive than men, you know? It's biologically proven. Especially when one mentions their kids."

The director glared at him. He had a certain pride in his eyes.

"These kids. They also happen to be yours, right?"

"You son-of—"

"Yeah. Life is a bitch. Now if you'd sign under this list, we can get you out of here in no time."

Pa handed him a list of names. The Hollywood director's chin trembled; he was ready to cry. As he signed the paper, he broke down.

I looked at him from behind the glass, impressed. Just then, Pa turned around and looked at me for a second, winked mischievously, and smiled a sweet smile.

When we left the building, we weren't singing. We never talked about that day. He never asked me to go see another confession. I never asked, either.

Through the week that followed the theft of Pa's watch, I had tracked and observed Dmitri on foot every day, trying to understand his personality and his secret to conquering fear. I had taken notes in my notebook. I wrote:

Loose, washed jackets that look European, charcoal gray

pants and worn-out, tight, sleeveless T-shirts. He walks waddling, feet dragging, lazy back. His favorite food, the same as his favorite fish to catch: yellowtail.

I felt kind of creepy carrying out this voyeuristic task. His way of standing was strange, kind of leaning to one side. I still wonder if that means something. I couldn't write much, though: he stayed on his boat most of the time, leaving it only to slouch to the market or to church every morning. I was disappointed because I didn't catch him stealing any watches.

I wrote: *A thief who believes in God.*

Me? I don't believe in anything, not even myself.

I needed to know more about Dmitri, but I didn't really want to meet him because I had so many expectations for my character—I was afraid the real Dmitri wouldn't turn out the way I imagined him. There was only one way to find out: investigate what people thought of him.

At the San Pedro harbor bar, I asked sailors and bums if they knew him.

"Dmitri? Of course, I know him," said a short man with jumpy eyes.

"Me too. He's a good friend," said a cowboy.

"He's from Russia," added another guy.

"No," said the cowboy, "Dmitri's father, who abandoned him, was from Russia."

"You have the story all wrong," yelled the bartender, "Dmitri told me he's originally from Oregon, but his mother, who abandoned him at a convent, was Russian."

"But he told me a different story," insisted the man with the jumpy eyes.

About his childhood and his obsession with the church I heard various stories—that he was abandoned in a church, that he had grown up in a church . All the tales were different. Dmitri had been telling a different version to each person.

I never thought I could trust him—after all he was an inventor of stories, like myself. His friends at the bar told me they knew he was a liar. What I didn't understand is why everybody adored him anyway. I told them I didn't care if he lied, but the truth was I didn't care as long as he didn't lie to me.

At home, I lay in bed with my eyes open and hesitated about my choice of character. Dmitri and I were different. He knew how to wait. I didn't know how to wait. He lived on his boat. I lived in the city. I hated nature. He lived on the docks, he lived on the water, among the slippery fish and sticky seaweed. I hated animals, plants, insects, living things, any being that could approach me.

Still, Dmitri was all I wanted to be. As I saw him, he was fearless and free because he was an orphan. He had no family, no one who had influenced his past. No one to blame for his failures, like I did.

My room was covered with notes about him taped to the walls, words written horizontally and vertically on little pieces of paper. There was a list of adjectives about him, all crossed out. A list of synonyms and antonyms to describe him. There were books all over—several by T.S. Eliot—their margins filled with handwriting. No words fit him.

I stopped writing and kicked the food that was on the floor—cookies, candy, cans. I wondered if I would ever really write about him, if I could really sound like him having the past I've had. Over and over I reviewed the notes in my notebook—not enough material for a big piece. With choking frustration, I thought about adding other pasts to his story. So I took a white sheet of paper, and I wrote in first person as if I were he, inventing for him the past I wanted.

I never knew why my mother called me Dmitri. For sure not after a saint. There are no Russian saints. My name is all I know about her. I was born in Oregon during a windy winter storm. It was a disastrous storm. A lot of people died. At least that's what the nuns told me when I was a kid. Although nuns make up stories. It was so cold the day I was born that my mother had to leave me there in the church because it was warmer. She left the bundle next to some potted paper-whites. The nuns told me this too. What I didn't understand is why she never came back. The nuns told me she was going to come back, and I waited and waited. I never believed the nuns, but I waited just in case. The only person in the whole church I could trust was the one standing naked up in front of the altar all day with his wooden eyes. I trusted him because he was a son too. I stayed many hours asking him questions about life that he never answered. But at least he listened. He paid attention. He stared at me. Nuns don't look you in the eye, not even when you talk to them. When I was nineteen years old, I decided to leave the church. I've always hated its orange-colored floor tiles. I stole a wonderful, small portrait of Jesus from the church. When I left, I wasn't looking for my mother. I was running from the idea that she would never come back. Back then, I had to travel to stop the fear. I have no fear now. I'm not attached to anyone. No one can get into me. Although a silent disdain follows me, and an overwhelming sadness grows within me, hard as dry grass.

Changing his past wasn't a crime; after all, I had made him better. I could almost feel as if I understood the character I'd created. Once I finished, he could become respectable. But in order to have a rounded story, I needed more material about him. If I wanted to finish the story, I had to get to know him.

Indigo Blue and Beige

On the hospital TV a program shows Monte Carlo's port, and I can't help but wonder about other ports.

"This hospital is sick," I mumble. "Any minute now, I'll go to my car and get the hell out of here. I don't remember where I put the keys, though."

I hate people who talk in the visitor's waiting room. There's a fat, sad woman with an El Salvador accent who complains about her grandmother's stomach and a bitter Mexican man who pronounces the "r" too much as he mentions his ulcer. Hospitals are filled with crazy, rambling people. Also, I hate the long, silver-plated fifties lamp I have in my room; the lamp is too old. I don't know why I'm here. I feel all right. I vomit and spit blood sometimes, but that's all. I can vomit whenever I want to; I put my fingers in my throat and touch deep inside me. In fact, I am perfectly all right. Besides, some days I don't even need painkillers; I learned to swallow pain a long time ago.

Sometimes I feel a little ache in my chest, but I haven't told the doctors about it. Mainly, I don't avoid pain, I learn from it. I use pain to control what I can't control inside me, like I use colors. A woman clutching a navy blue sweater passes by on the street, two locked, ink blue cars—three—another sky blue car—four blues.

"I know how to hot-wire cars," the kid mutters from his bed.

"I know exactly where the key to my car is. What? Do

you think I got Alzheimer's? Well, I don't. It's just that I don't remember because of the medicine they give me. They do it on purpose."

"I know it's not your fault," the kid removes some wires from the fifties lamp and starts peeling them back with a plastic knife. "I can help you get out. Trust me."

"I only trust Leukemia, because she does her work on time."

"I have to get out of here, too, you see? To find my father to celebrate Christmas."

"But it's July."

"So?"

I look curiously at the kid as he braids the wires; he knows what he's doing. "Maybe we could do a kind of trade, if you promise me I can escape with you," the kid whispers. "Where are you planning to go?"

On television an adventurous ship raises its sails and drifts freely. "I want to get to the harbor." I feel a hollowness inside my chest. "There's one thing I have to do before next week . . . before . . . no way I'm going with you."

I look at the four walls that surround me. If I stay here, I can only wait for it to happen. All old people do is wait for death. Some old people might sit on a park bench and talk to the other old folks, do puzzles or play chess, go to the movies at 11 A.M., go every day to the same bar and order the same food. People my age can take three hours to have breakfast. These old people go where there's sun or air conditioning and wait until *the day*—until death comes to wake them up. Not me. I'm almost seventy, but I feel like sixty, maybe sixty-two. I'm going to go out there to search for my beige friend Death.

———

Night has climbed the window. We wait until the hospital is completely quiet—close to quiet because in hospitals time is not normal—death doesn't care whether it's day or night. Almost everybody is sleeping, but strange screaming comes from the end of the corridor. Moaning, gurgling like dying. I haven't slept very well lately. For me, sleeping, like falling in love, has always been a waste of time.

As the kid helps me get out of bed, I can't stand as well as I thought, although my knees aren't that weak. Maybe I'm just a little stiff. I reach out for the door knob and scratch my arm on it, but nothing too bad. We leave our pillows under the sheets like in the movies—that was the kid's idea.

We don't have clothes to change into—they took them away—so we walk through the corridors in our turquoise green hospital pajamas. The kid mumbles that the color green is sad. We have no shoes, so we walk barefoot. The floor has absorbed the coolness of the night.

A nurse passes by. We slip in and out of the shadows and hide in a small closet, warily. The kid is scared; I don't have anything to lose if they catch me. Inside the dark closet he takes my hand. His hand is clammy. I hate holding hands, so I take mine away.

We don't use the front elevator since there are two fat, vicious orderlies on duty in the reception area. Escaping from the fluorescent lights of the corridor, we sneak to the outside stairs. On our way down, I slip just three times and catch myself on the banister. Not bad for my condition.

I take my medical chart with me. Clinical words are written all over it, but the doctors don't understand *me*. They counted my red globules, they counted my white globules, but they didn't get it. They only added up colors like I do.

We open the exit door and the night air reveals itself in all its darkness. I know, like the night, to camouflage myself when the colors around me are darker than the bottom of the ocean.

We finally make it to the small parking lot. It is deserted and dark, but on the pavement small particles gleam and flicker as if they are moving. In the security booth, a guard sleeps with a magazine over his face.

In the cold, the kid approaches the dashboard with a plastic knife and the points of two wires. The engine starts. It works. Great. For a moment, I am not sure if this is my car; all these small, Japanese cars look the same. This is an indigo blue Toyota, like mine, but I can't tell. Then I recognize the little purple-red sugar packets on the floor and a bottle of painkillers.

The guard lifts his head. We kneel down, hiding our own. He doesn't see us. Cautiously I slide into the front seat and search in the glove compartment for a lipstick; I find one melted by the sun. It makes sense that I have to look good if I am going out, so I slide it over my wrinkled upper lip. Funeral pink makes me look smashing.

When I move the floor shifter, the radio begins to play new-generation music, so I switch it off. Who the hell changed my dial? I'm glad I have an automatic, perfect for old people. I hardly have to move. Besides, I never use neutral or reverse. If one is going to die, it is better to die moving ahead.

A helicopter flies above us and its spotlight dashes around. Slowly we get out of the hospital parking lot.

"How long since you saw the sailor?" the kid asks.

"I haven't seen him in more than thirty years."

"For how long exactly?"

"Forty-nine."

"Maybe he's not even there."

"He has to be. I only have a week to tell him something."

Steel Gray

We pass Alisitos, Plaza del Mar, Puerto Nuevo, Ensenada. I drive Tijuana by heart like I know the place, although I haven't been here in ages. Music blasts from the different little stores. As we pass by, one song melts into the next. Margaritas, tamales, and burritos are advertised. When I stop at a red light, I look out the window and see some guys in baseball caps drinking orange juice and eating tacos outside a twenty-four-hour Mexican joint. They seem so overly happy it makes me sick. I just can't stand orange juice. Why does everybody drink orange juice?

An annoying, seventies Mustang honks behind me. "Calm down, goon, I've already seen the green light." I drive slowly, I know, and I can't get to the pedals like I used to—my legs are shorter than before. I don't want to rush because I haven't driven in a long time. The kid stares at me. I know he's going to ask one of those difficult questions.

"Goon is an old-fashioned word. You should try dummy or asshole. Maybe even idiot."

"Look here, you're not going to teach me how to talk." Mumbling the song "You Are My Sunshine," I push the pedal harder, and the kid falls back against the seat.

"Where are we going?" he asks.

"First I have to return a couple of books to the Tijuana library. I've had them for seventeen years; I just remembered them. They're going to charge me a fortune. I hope the library didn't move. . . . Well, I guess they can wait a couple of days, until I come back."

We pass wig stores, mango and fruit carts, and two-dollar-margarita joints.

"Where are we going?" the kid scratches the scars on his cheeks.

I hate people who repeat questions. Kids repeat questions all the time and don't get bored if you tell them the same story over and over. As I put on my best annoyed face, I roll my eyes and answer, "North. Although to go north, we also go a bit east."

"How far north?"

"Look kid, you can get out wherever you want."

"But you promised I could go with you. You promised! You promised!"

"All right, all right, shut up!"

We meet a freeway, and I decide not to take it. I prefer surface streets; freeways are too fast for me, too modern. Caged streets and alleys make me feel in control.

We pass a Peugeot with leopard-skin seats and a truck with a tropical painting on the hood. When we cross the Avenida Independencia, I realize I can't remember how far north I am actually going, which harbor I have to go to. I feel a little dizzy. I just can't remember which port. Really, I can't. I stop the car.

Out of breath, I look around desperately. When I see what I need in a store, I get out of the car and walk around to the passenger side. The kid tries to follow me, but I quickly close the door on his face.

"Don't get out. I'll be right back."

———

Using all my strength, I open the heavy door of the gun store; an innocent bell clangs. The walls are lined with shelves of dark wood, and some of them have glass doors. Inside, all kinds of guns. Steel gray gleams out of the glass. Slowly I walk towards the front counter. A huge, rusty machine gun stands on display. It looks like the ones you see on television. I have never seen a real one before.

"¡Hola!" someone yells, and it scares the hell out of me.

"Hello?" I answer with my best American accent. I refuse to speak awful Mexican Spanish. I would speak Castillian Spanish, but I don't think anyone here would understand me.

"Yello!" hollers the broken-English voice from behind the shelves. Then a short, olive-colored man emerges from a small door in the floor. "Can I help you?"

"No. I was just looking."

I majestically glance to my side and check out the machine gun. No, not a machine gun. They're too heavy; I couldn't carry it. Mine has to be small, pocket-size—a lady's size, I guess—and very elegant.

Intrigued, I look at the guns under the glass of the counter. The color of these guns is more opaque, dull, not so flashy. One has to take care of one's good taste at all times.

The short man stares at me, waiting. A bit worried, I wonder if he can guess what I am planning. He doesn't say a word. So, I don't either.

I move my eyes closer to another glass cabinet. These are small ones. Some are rectangular and some have a barrel. I prefer the barreled ones—they seem to match my age better.

I'm about to point at a gun, but I stop myself. Suddenly I am suspicious of the old guns. Maybe they are too old and won't fire. How old is too old?

Right then, I point at a small-barreled gun with a leather grip, and he hands it to me. Cautiously I move it from one hand to the other; I feel its delightful weight. Pointing the gun at the guy, I say, "Can you shoot a person from twenty feet with this gun?"

"I guess you could, Ma' am" the short man says, backing away. He trembles a little, but not enough. Looking through the pistol's sight, I have him at gun point.

"Miss," I say.

"Sorry . . . Miss."

"Can you kill a lot of people at the same time, or just one at a time?"

"Are you going to do all these things?"

"Just checking," I sneer sternly. "Do you think this is a lady's model?"

"Of course, it's light and pocket-size. Do you know how to use it?"

"Yeah."

"Because it's very dangerous if you don't . . ."

"I learned on TV."

"Do you have a permit to carry it?"

"I'm kind of in a hurry. How much would it be without a permit?"

He smiles broadly. I turn around, take a bunch of wrinkled bills from my pocket, and deposit the wad on the table. "So how much for the lady's gun?"

"For you I'm going to set a special price, because women at your age shouldn't be without protection."

"Men of your height, either." He doesn't smile, but I do as I grab my gun.

As soon as I get in the car, I quickly put the paper bag with the gun into the glove compartment and politely wink at the kid. "Women's stuff I had to take care of. Shall we continue our nice trip?"

Military Olive Green

Heaps of fish with bellies laid open, massive anchors, and an array of skulls made the Port of San Pedro hideous with sights and smells of death. It was late fall; the weather was sticky cold. Navy ships' hulls were being loaded with olive green military equipment. At the side of the wharf, a flock of soldiers was trying to convince a couple of fortune tellers to make love to them, while two photographers were taking pictures of the little fish stalls. No one looked at the ocean.

My purpose was to be as tall as he was, or at least not any shorter, and I tried to disguise my nineteen years in high heels. My brown leather high heels matched my large, man's zoot suit, which hung over my tiny shoulders, so only the tips of my fingers showed below the sleeves. So I walked onto the docks with my chin up and went straight to the wharf where his boat was tied. I had decided I had to stop guessing and find out for myself—what he thought, why he stole *only* watches. Maybe he knew the secret relativity of time. Maybe he didn't believe in time. Maybe he was against time, like I was. Maybe he was like me in some way.

I had planned for all the possibilities: if he denied being a thief, I would say I was going to call the police, and he would have to talk. To give myself strength I walked stubbornly, straightening up my back like an ironing board.

When I got there, he was cleaning a gray fish on the wooden wharf next to his boat. As only an expert would do, he flipped the fish over, revealing its golden belly.

"Hello," I muttered.

He filleted the fish and glanced up at me, nodding. Then he noticed my expensive man's suit and grinned. I noticed his dirty clothes and sneered, shivering inside. Because I had waited for this moment for so long, the words dried up like winter leaves in my throat. I wondered if he realized I was intimidated by him.

"Great name," I said, looking at "Suzy" painted in yellow letters on the side of the boat. "So, who was this Suzy? A love story?"

"No. I didn't love her . . ." he said in a tender lazy voice with an strange, deep accent. "but she taught me how to write her name, so I painted it on the front of my boat."

I felt relieved because I didn't want any women interrupting my work. Then I stared at the short nails on his toes. I wasn't sure if he had recognized me from the bar, so I unbrushed my hair with my fingers.

"I want to know about the watches. Why don't you sell them?"

He looked behind me suspiciously, as if checking to see if someone had followed me.

"If you don't tell me I'll call the police . . . or the Committee. Are you Russian? Or un-American? Is that it?"

Before I could say anything more, he picked up a fish from the pile and said with a serene, almost lazy, voice, "Look, I steal watches because I like watches and I want to have them." He calmly grabbed the fish's tail and started to clean it. "They're easy to steal. I like easy things."

It sounded reasonable. But he wasn't against time, like I

thought. He didn't say more. He didn't introduce himself, but he also didn't tell me to leave.

I looked at him with a mixture of fascination and fear. His droopy blond hair fell over his earnest face as he unrolled a piece of black velvet on the dock and spread out the watch collection he carried in his big jacket pockets. He showed me a lady's Cartier wristwatch, a white-gold Rolex, a baguette-shaped Omega, a diamond-squared Dunhill, a Longines bracelet, and other, newer brands. He had about thirty watches, and I searched for mine but didn't see it. He pointed at them proudly, as if he were a pirate showing me his treasure.

"Wow," I grinned. "Do you have to synchronize them all?"

He didn't know what "synchronize" meant.

"To get the same hour . . ."

He said that having all the watches show the same time would be stupid. I asked him what he meant.

"One day I wanted to know what time it was in London, so I stole an English watch. The same with a Swiss Zenith. Now I know what time it is in many countries of the world. In case someone asks."

Why not just add and subtract hours instead of carrying around all these watches? I assumed his math wasn't very good.

"I use the watches depending on my mood," he said. "There are times when I want to feel calm so I wear an Egyptian watch; if I need to rush things or be precise, I wear my Japanese Seiko."

Further down the wharf a patrol car chased a man, the siren wailing, and people were running in all directions. We both froze. Howls. Screams. Lights. Chaos.

We jumped into the boat. I tripped over a rope, lost my footing and almost fell, but grabbed on to the mast. The siren moaned. Dmitri grabbed my shoulder; I flinched and pulled back. He shoved me down, and we knelt, trying to hide ourselves with an unused sail. We stayed still, our heads down, hands over our ears, scared eyes gazing at each other. Silent eyes. Close. Too close. His eyes made goose bumps high up on my arms, as if I had sand under my skin. I couldn't stand his gaze, so I peeked out from under the sail and focused on an olive green barnacle growing on the wharf.

When the siren stopped, Dmitri suggested that we wait a few minutes and I noticed that his hand was still on my shoulder. It was dark under the sail, but because we were near, I saw his eyes at close range. Still, I couldn't define their color.

Outside, people started chatting and walking around again, so we got out from underneath the sail.

"You can go now," he said.

"Why? Won't you invite me to come in? That's not very polite."

Not very convinced, he invited me in. It was a small, asphyxiating sardine can of a boat where there was a cramped chart table, a little bed, a stove, and a tiny bathroom. Dirty clothes, marine magazines, comic books, cards, and dominoes were scattered all over the floor. A phonograph with its front broken. Brown wooden walls, wooden furniture. I wondered how he would describe the place:

> My boat has the furniture of a country house, not of a boat, and I put amber lamps on the deck that give a yellow

color to the water. Yellow mixed with the blue of the ocean ends up a light green, which is always better than red mixed with blue that would make the water purple.

I always hated boats. The sensation of not being on firm ground made me feel not in control. You never know what to expect from boats. I winced at the mess, but I didn't want to invade his privacy, so I just stared at the ocean chart.

"Let me introduce myself. I'm a writer," I cleared my voice, and, I, uh, want to write about you. If you let me observe you, I can give you some money."

He didn't say a word and began cleaning his watches with a toothbrush. I felt so awkward that I decided to write his answer in my notebook:

Sure, I can use the money, and I wouldn't mind looking at your sad beauty more often.

"Sorry. You have rust on your face," he pointed at my cheek.

My notes didn't always have to be faithful to his words. I cleaned the red rust stain with the palm of my hand.

"Why write about me?"

"I think you're interesting. Tell me more about yourself. Anything."

"I don't know how to talk about myself."

"Well, talk about the watches and all, where you've been, your favorite country, what you like. I don't know . . ."

"Well, I've been all over. I don't have a favorite place. Maybe the Mediterranean, which is transparent, warm, and truthful. Or the Indian, which is darkest with the thickest water. Or the Pacific, which is the deepest blue, the coldest blue. You see, I'm always moving. I move more swiftly than the water and more anxiously than the dust."

"Robbing and traveling. Are you looking to live a high-risk life?"

"I move when I want to, that's all," he grumbled, polishing a Cartier. "For example, next week I'm going to sail to Mexico." He paused, "So you won't be able to write about me. I don't think you'll wanna come, do you?"

"Sailing? I don't think so." I wondered about his strange accent, a mix of accents from all the countries he had visited, an accent that belonged nowhere. We remained discreetly silent.

I scratched in my notebook the part about the oceans, and I came back to the part I liked . . . *your sad beauty.*

He kept on cleaning a watch with a pearl bezel on its cage. He didn't even glance at me.

"I can write about you when you come back. When will you be back?"

"Never," he growled, leaving the watches. I began to arrange the dominoes and the charts on the shelves. He lazily looked at my dirty finger, spotted with ink; I looked at his—perfectly clean. I hid mine.

He might be escaping something or someone, I thought. On the other hand, I hated to sail, so I asked him why he had to go by boat and not by car, to which he answered, "I never was behind the wheel. Only at the helm."

My perfect character was about to disappear. I felt lost, but worse than that. I agonizingly looked at the wrinkles of my skirt. Outside, the intimidating water softly slapped the boat. I really hated the harbor's silence.

While he polished the watches, his pastel pink lips hummed something I couldn't understand. A song? Where from? I didn't ask. He was sitting on a magazine to keep me from seeing it. I cautiously moved my head to look: a comic book with a big-breasted, long-haired woman. He probably felt embarrassed that he wasn't reading a real book.

"I have written things for magazines. I like them, too," I said to share something with him. And then I thought that maybe if he liked how I wrote, he would stay.

On a napkin I wrote out a short poem I was planning to publish in a literary magazine, and I handed it to him.

"This is a poem I wrote a few years ago. Read it when you have time and tell me what you think. Although you can read it now if you want."

"Now?"

"Why not?"

He grabbed the napkin. I read it over his shoulder while the national anthem played on the radio.

I want to breathe fewer words or none.
My world is a gray cumulus cloud,
my bloodless body a dry leaf,
and my face a name I can't remember.

While he looked at it again incredulously, I checked around and noticed a few dried flowers in an empty beer bottle.

"It's all right," he said.

"Just all right? But it's the best thing I've ever written."

We stayed quiet for a long time; I don't remember how long, but I think I listened to two whole songs on his radio. He didn't talk; I didn't talk. A fly entered the cabin and traveled around the room, buzzing softly. I observed it, following it as it made circles. It landed on my arm, and I watched it cleaning its legs. I counted the colors on its wings—green, black, yellow, orange. Suddenly I smashed it with my thumb, watching its legs shake, fast at the first, then one trembling, until it stopped.

Proudly I lifted my eyes and smiled at him, and he looked at me with a strange expression. The boat started to rock. The front cabin looked close and then far, far and then close, and I started to feel as sick as a long-lost bottle drifting in the water.

I had nothing more to say. I really wanted to leave and to run—to stop this stupid obsession with a man I didn't know. The floor of the boat was brown. I didn't leave.

What I hated the most was how he stared deeply into my eyes, as if he were waiting for some kind of statement. I didn't know what he meant by those big silences, so I gave him a harsh look. Because of the scowl he gave back to me, I knew he didn't like my look.

What do I care about the way she looks at me? I hate her stare more than the color orange. I want to tell her what I'm thinking, but I can't find the words. I want to breathe fewer words or none.

"You scan me, searching for something, but I'm just this.

I'm just what you see," he mumbled. Then he stuffed something into a bag and said, "Sorry, lady, I have to leave now. Look, find someone else to write about."

We left the boat and stood on the wharf. He gave me one last cursory glance, and I stared back at him, waiting for words that never came. Then suddenly he left. Alone, I stared at his drab, olive green sail for a while. Maybe he really had something to do—he didn't say what, though. Maybe he was going fishing. Maybe he wasn't lying, but I liked the way I was writing him as a liar.

I didn't have a reason to leave anyway. Maybe he was really lying. "Go to hell, thief!" I yelled, about ten minutes after he had left. Two sailors from the next boat looked at me as if I were crazy. Then I realized I hadn't told him my name.

So I wrote my name on a piece of paper and tied it to the helm.

As if hypnotized, I stayed there gazing at a watch he had left on the table, a watch with a satin strap, and I thought about going to Mexico. With what money? How, if not by the boat? When? No. Impossible. I couldn't just leave my job and family. I wondered if Dmitri felt badly that he had left .

I walked for two blocks, and I decided to come back to talk to her. When I arrived, she was gone.

The truth is that I waited for two hours and twenty-three minutes on his boat, and he didn't return. So I decided I couldn't go to Mexico, yet I couldn't let him go, either.

Old Yellow

To numb the tourist noise of Tijuana, I follow the rhythm of the trumpets on the radio with my fingers, beating on the steering wheel. The shadows of the trees are drawn on the car window. The kid stares straight at me.

"With that shitty boat he went all the way to Japan and Switzerland to get watches? That's bullshit."

"I don't know why you doubt me. I don't lie."

"I'm tired of your old stories. I'm starving. All I have left is a piece of gum," he whines. "You should stop soon. I'm hungry! I wanna eat!"

The sun beats down through a cloudless sky. The lack of wind makes the heat even more oppressive. I push the gas pedal. I don't want to stop. I don't even answer the kid. The roadsides are white and dry as a salt desert. We have already lost time buying clothes with the money the kid found in my glove compartment.

The kid wears jean shorts and an emerald green T-shirt that bears the face of a disgusting rock 'n' roll singer. I bought a pale peach, practical summer dress that has a discreet, grape-colored floral pattern. I hate short sleeves, but the damned salesgirl said they are in fashion now. I definitely hate short sleeves.

"Shit," I mutter, looking angrily at the sleeves.

"You use bad words too much, ma'am."

"I may use bad words, but you know what? I'm never vulgar. I use them with class."

I fold over the short sleeves. Maybe he is right—I lose a lot of time hating. I hate something about everyone I meet: rebellious, messy hair, an awful facial tick, a color that doesn't match, an annoying word, an annoying kid. He keeps staring at me. I know exactly what he wants.

"Calm down," I tell him, "you're not going to die if you don't eat for five hours; believe me, I have experience. Once I spent five weeks without a bite, kid." Rearranging my body in the seat, I move my back, which hurts a little. The kid notices this.

"Here, you have a knob that makes the seat lean back and forward," he turns the knob. The seat moves and it feels so much better.

"Thanks, kid."

"Stop calling me kid. My name is Juan," he pouts.

"I don't care. I'm gonna call you kid because you're the only kid I've ever talked to, and besides, I don't want to get to know you." I hear him chewing his gum. "I drive with you because I promised you I would. And a promise is a promise. But I don't need your company. I can drive with any kid in the world. Or without kids. Is that clear?"

The kid nods. I know I'm strict with him, but I have to be. Messy things happen when people get to know each other.

"Patience is the word," I tell him, emphasizing the slow movement of my hand as I speak. When I was young, patience helped me wait until the screenplay was really ready to be filmed. And I waited and waited, and one day I realized I was thirty and it wasn't perfect. Then I realized I was sixty and it still wasn't perfect. "I hate to repeat it, kid, but patience is the strength of wise, elderly people." I realize I'm getting old when I start giving advice nobody asked for. I know patience didn't take me anywhere, but what can I say to a young kid? Patience is shit, time is shit, wisdom is shit? I can't tell him that. "Maybe I have some money for candy," I tell him instead and pull over to the roadside.

I glance around to check if anybody is nearby. A thief or someone. No car stops. It seems like everyone is in a hurry, just fast-colored shadows crossing the road. The jade green bushes are moved by the wind from the cars. The edges of the road gleam like mirrors. Then I open my butter cream purse. The first thing I see is a mint candy, so I hand it to the kid.

"I don't like mint," he growls. I glare at him angrily. He excuses himself, "But I think I might like mint when I get older. The same with wine, cigarettes, and coffee."

I search through my purse and find a picture of my family when I was young. My parents always smiled in pictures, never in real life. I had my hair done in curls for the occasion, a pearl necklace and pearl earrings, tight skin and blush on my cheeks. I think I looked pretty then. "See kid, I wasn't always like this. I looked normal once," I give him the picture.

He stares at it. "Yes. I've seen this kind of picture. Pictures of people that are now dead. A bunch of baldies and a few ugly girls who seem dull and stupid looking. They all wear brown clothes and dummy smiles."

I take the picture from his hand and again check the empty road just in case a thief appears, but of course no one does, not even a butterfly. As I keep on looking for money in my purse, I find the last letter I wrote to Dmitri, which I never sent. It's old and yellow-colored. "After the last day I saw him, I wrote him several letters. In the letters, I explained to him why I did what I did, why I left. Through the years, I kept throwing away each letter to write a better one, a clearer one, and another, and another, until I finally gave up. Since 1953 I have written him 184 letters. And one day I finally stopped. I kept just the last one."

"What does it say?" the kid asks.

"Nothing I would say now." I crumple up the letter and throw it out the window.

"What happened then? He sailed to Mexico and you . . . ?"

"To know what happened, you'll have to listen to the rest of the story. I'll tell you later."

"Tell me now."

"I don't know . . ."

"C'mon . . ."

"Since I couldn't let him go, I had a week to convince him to stay."

"Ahhh . . ." The kid rolls over on the back seat.

On the black asphalt of the road, little droplets of water shine. By 6 A.M. we pass a sign that says: Mexico/United States Border 30 Miles.

In the U.S., I'm gonna find him. He has to be there. I don't feel like nineteen, though. My eyes are dimmer and my back is bent at the waist, but I'm going to keep driving until I arrive. All this driving is not going to kill me.

I see on the dashboard that the gas tank reads empty, I skip over the letter, and search for my wallet. In it, a couple of old business cards from probably dead people, a small piece of paper with an address written on it and a five-dollar bill.

"Great. I thought I had more money; we spent everything on these awful clothes. Just great."

"We'll need more gas if we plan to cross the border."

"Who the hell gave me the idea of going somewhere? With only five dollars we'll never get to the past."

Once in a while, I unfasten and refasten my seat belt to be sure I am safe.

Wild Reds

Two burgundy tablecloths, one bottle of cabernet sauvignon: three reds. Plus one small, red flag on the wall of the seedy Italian canteen: four reds.

Four locals drank beer and sang sailors' songs. Looking stubborn, Dmitri was wearing a striped blue and white sleeveless T-shirt. To match the harbor ambiance, I had bought a white sailor's cap. We were sitting at the same table, but he didn't look at me. He acted as if I were invisible, but I knew he was thinking about me, so I wrote what I thought it was in his mind:

> I like it that she followed me here, that she won't leave me.
> I'm not afraid of her gaze like I'm not afraid of winds.

He interrupted my writing. "Why don't you leave me alone? Why would anyone want to write about me?"

"I said I could pay you," I handed him some money cautiously since I had never paid a man for anything.

"You just paid for the food," he took the money from my hand so fast I didn't see it disappear. As he turned around to the kitchen and licked his lips, I went back to writing, wondering why he would like this seedy place.

> I like this restaurant. The mix of colors. Its smell: the mix
> of coffee, salty wind, and people's noble sweat when they
> smell like fear.

"Why do you like this place?" I asked him, to check if my

vision of him was correct.

"I like to come here because it's near my boat and the owner treats me like I'm family. Plus there's always a bunch of sailors eating here who like to shoot the breeze."

Pretty close to my description, I thought incorrectly, and scribbled down more words. When I raised my head from the page, I saw two FBI agents eating oily fried eggs and staring at me. I knew what those guys looked like and recognized them because they wore the typical FBI brown suits.

"They are probably looking for un-Americans," I whispered to Dmitri.

"You mean, Americans who have their own opinions."

From their table, far away, the agents looked at me, whispered something, and laughed. I scowled, made an ugly gesture with my nose, and said almost to myself, "What? What the hell is going on with you guys? You don't like my cap? What do you know about hats anyway?"

"Would you stop that?" Dmitri whispered. "They're going to come after me, and then I'm the one who'll have to fight. I don't want any problems with the FBI. Not now."

Not now? Why not? I didn't ask him. He put a blue bandanna over his forehead, carefully hiding his blond hair.

"Okay. I thought I could get by unnoticed if I wore something typically marine." I took my damned hat off.

A fat and pimpled waiter came to the table, dragging his feet and whistling.

"Three yellowtail sandwiches," Dmitri smiled at him, showing the gap between his teeth. Then he looked at me, "I only eat fish. The rest upsets my stomach."

Fish in a sandwich? I had never heard of the combination. Three sandwiches? To me, people who ate too much had other vices.

"A salad, please." I ordered a salad because all Italian pasta sauces look orange.

I must have scowled again, I guess, because Dmitri looked annoyed. "What are you thinking? Tell me the truth," I asked.

"Nothing."

"Tell me."

"Nothing. It's the truth. You know, sometimes people don't like to hear the truth. I always say the truth, even if people glare at me." He opened his nostrils. While he talked, I wrote what I wanted him to say, using some of his words.

> I always tell the truth. All writers are liars, because they need written words to express their feelings. If she lies, I can lie too. And tell her I tell the truth. . . .

"I always tell the truth . . . I can't help it," he said. "Sometimes I have problems; some people don't like to hear the truth. I don't need people anyway. I can talk to the sea or to my boat. It's just me and my boat." He stared at me. "Did you write that? Me and my boat." He picked his nose while I was taking notes on everything he said and everything I thought he thought. "Me and my boat," he repeated, "I think that's poetry."

You have no idea what poetry is, Dmitri, I thought. I stared at him, traveling through his cheek, his chapped-by-the-sun lips and the dark blue shadow of his eyelashes, and still I couldn't tell if his eyes were gray or blue . . .

The agents stood up and walked to the bathroom. Dmitri watched them leave, waited a few seconds, and followed them.

Because I didn't like to be left alone, I locked myself in my notebook:

Just one fall afternoon with you
Can make me spit words for hours
And sweat your name for days.
You, the balance of my time,
Wanted to play without knowing the end of the game.
Not knowing that is the only way to play.
Now I would only like to faint
With your smile in my mouth.

Maybe it was very melodramatic. I would describe it as a wild poem, a burgundy poem. I didn't know where it came from because I didn't care about anyone. Faked feelings, all in the name of art. But I felt dizzier than in the boat, so I took a deep breath. I felt a feeling in my stomach similar to fear. This was surely a feeling which I didn't have a word for, and I had no idea where it had come from, or what it was. Moreover, I didn't know if I should store this feeling along with my hatred.

Dmitri came back from the bathroom and sat down. I couldn't look at him because I was worried the queasy feeling would translate to my face.

After I reread the poem, a sadness came over me, so I started counting again: two burgundy tablecloths, one bottle of cabernet sauvignon, one small, red flag on the wall of the restaurant, one ugly kid with a carmine T-shirt. You could say five reds.

I stared at the ugly kid, who was picking his nose. To open the conversation with Dmitri again, I told him, "I hate kids."

He said, "I want to have six or eight of my own," and there our conversation finished for the rest of lunch. Our friendship was broken before it had ever started. Outside, a dark cloud covered the water. A rusty buoy rocked quietly in the deep silence; not in our silence but in another more dense, more foreign.

When he had finished his three sandwiches, I asked him, "What time is it in Italy now?" I wanted to force a conversation and I knew he always carried his watches in his big jacket pockets.

To my astonishment, he took out a bunch of them under the table and proudly picked a gold-banded Gucci: "Eleven to nine."

"A.M. or P.M.?"

"P.M."

I imagined what I would be doing by 11 P.M. if I were in Italy. Probably eating or writing or reading, just like any other hour in any other country of the world. I asked myself why people need to travel, why they need to change.

And then I used my secret tactic to make him stay. What else? Show him what I had written. I knew the poem I had shown him on the boat hadn't worked, but I thought that if he liked the way I described him, it would get to his ego and he would stay.

"This is the first scene of my screenplay. Take a peek. I want to get your opinion."

I gave him the pages solemnly. He looked hastily at the first paragraph and said, "The beginning is nice. I'll read the rest later."

Just nice? I guess he didn't have too many words to explain what my words produced in him. Yet I thought he liked it, because I liked it, so I swallowed bitterly the intimation of my lack of greatness.

Another FBI agent entered the restaurant and headed to the bar. Dmitri's eyes became a little edgy, and he said we had to leave. So we hid under the table, and when the agent turned around, we hurriedly sneaked out of the place. I didn't ask why.

On our way out of the restaurant, Dmitri showed me two watches he had stolen from the FBI agents in the bathroom. An Omega official timekeeper from the 1936 Olympic Games and a Breitling RAF watch that was supplied to U.S. servicemen during World War II.

He walked proudly; I, paranoid, glancing watchfully from side to side. Curiously, I felt like a thief's partner, although I had to admit this event gave me the adrenaline I needed for my screenplay, but not for myself. Stealing was fun, but I personally didn't want to go to jail. My goal wasn't to be a thief; all I wanted was not to be me.

―――

During the days that followed, I worked in the morning and went to the harbor on my lunch break, walking among the fish and hangover smells. The San Pedro marina wasn't like others—it had colorful bars, pizza parlors, nostalgic people. Usually I just showed up and stepped onto his boat without knocking. He never knew when I was going to appear. It was always a surprise. Although I loved surprises, I don't know if he liked them. Sometimes he would smile when I arrived. Not always. Other times he flared his nostrils. I prefer to remember only the days he smiled.

In my head I have a picture, like a Rembrandt painting, of him smiling at the cabin door. I didn't want life to be like art; I wanted life to be art.

He fished. I wrote. He had beers with the sailors; everybody at the marina knew him. No one knew me. He had lots of friends at the pier. I had him. He liked to remain silent. I made him talk.

I wrote more than had ever been written in the history of the world, I filled almost half of my notebook with magical moments and completed several scenes. I didn't stop to eat, I didn't stop to sleep. When I was awake, I saw things only to record them in my notebook, and only left home to go the port to fill myself with more of him. Every time I left him, I felt a strange pain, a sharp sting under my ribs.

I attributed this productive writing process to him, and I kept giving him all I wrote, even though he never made comments. I didn't care, because I felt I had become a real writer. With him, a complete person. The words just came into my head from a place outside of myself, as if I were another individual. Or a character. As if I were *he*. The problem was that later on I really thought I *was* he.

Chocolate Brown

About two hundred feet from the Mexico/U.S. border, we stopped the car. We have no money. We have no gas.

When I crossed this border fifty years ago there were marigolds on the path. Now they have cactus and a big, steel gray fence. What happened to the damned marigolds?

We wait on the Mexican side, longingly looking at the border. Behind the immigration booth, an endless stream of dreadful people forming lines to be free. I know the Americans are against me because I'm coming back. I can't prove it, but I know it. I know they hate me.

A tall, American officer dressed in coffee brown is at one of the border booths. He orders silence in English, but no one in the line understands. Mexicans dressed in bright colors beg and yell, and finally swear, to enter the freest country in the world. In America you can be whatever you always dreamed you wanted to be, or at least you can allow yourself to dream. There are no millionaire dreams in Mexico because there's no money to make them come true. How does one live dreamless?

The kid looks at me in awe. "This is where our deal ends, kid. You're going to have to stay here. You're a minor. They're never gonna let you cross the border without your folks. Do you even have a passport on you?"

"Does that guy look like my father?" the kid points to a Mexican with a thick mustache and sideburns who clutches a gleaming leather portfolio.

I look suspiciously at the black eyes of the Mexican and then at the kid's sage green eyes, "No way."

"How about that other one?" he points to a skinny, young, redheaded man, "Does he look like me?"

I glance at the kid's black hair and shake my head no. Being here again makes me feel caged. I button up the last button of the dress at my neck. As I move my shoulders up and down, my vertebrae make noise; I can't sit too long, if I sit too long my back aches. Trying to distract myself from pain, I look in the mirror; my face wrinkles like an accordion.

Certain that I need to stretch my legs, I pull the car into the parking lot of the last Mexican minimart. On the window, many advertisements for the lottery and greasy food. No Snickers or Milky Ways made from only-God-knows-what; here they sell only real chocolate made from cocoa.

"Can I go into the market, please? I'm starving," the kid pouts at me with sad eyes.

"I'm not waiting for you. Say good-bye now."

"Come on . . ."

"Look, kid, we have no money for candy"

"I don't need money. I'm sure they'll give me chocolate if I giggle. I've done it before. Maybe I'll even get some gas money for you."

"All right. Go ahead."

He runs into the minimart, and I think of leaving him there and driving off.

As I see him run away, I get out of the car to stretch my legs, and my knee makes a cracking noise. Then I stand by the door and realize I'm shorter. My head used to pass

through the sun roof and now it doesn't. Son-of-a-bitch . . . !
I've shrunk. I must have lost a few inches.

I glance at my watch. For me, waiting is the worst thing,
so I start panting and grimacing. Dmitri's absence is present
for me, when I'm full of nothing. Fighting the idea of him, I
want to start counting colors, but I can't when he is on my
mind.

A guy with a silvery belt and cranberry red cowboy
boots walks behind me and mumbles a disgusting compli-
ment about my legs.

"Go to hell," I say. He's obviously connected to the
Americans who are now conspiring to keep me out of my
country like they kicked me out back then. He looks suspicious, somehow too normal.

I squint at the hospital pajamas in the back seat of the car
with a vengeance. The pajama sleeves are long enough to
strangle someone, I think.

Coughing a bit, I watch the people waiting in line to cross
the border. Just one thin line and you are in another world.
Cross the limit. How many times had I crossed the limit?
When I was a teenager, I believed I had crossed it when I read
Sigmund Freud, but then I read Marguerite Duras, and the
previous limit wasn't enough. At nineteen, I believed I
crossed the limit with Dmitri. Maybe I had. Now my bound-
ary is death, my limit is beneath the soil, deeper than tree
roots. I can do whatever I want with no consequences. I can
even run over that jerk with the cowboy boots, and nothing
would be different for me. I could kill hundreds of people. Or
just one.

The kid comes back running with a big paper bag in his arms. "Let's go!" he is yelling. "Let's go! Start the engine! Quick, come on! Drive this dinky car!"

I do what he says—even if I don't understand what dinky means—something is wrong. As I push the gas pedal, I can see some people in the rearview mirror yelling at me, including a guy with an apron with the market's logo.

"Damn, more members of the group that hate me."

"They don't hate you. They hate me."

"They hate you too? Damn."

I speed up towards the border and almost hit some Mexicans selling car insurance and sombreros. They swear at me in Spanish. "*La chingada, vieja de m . . .*" In the rearview mirror, I see their papers and hats flying.

"Hide under the seat, kid."

"I don't want to."

"Hide. I'm telling you. I don't have your papers, and if they hate you like they hate me, we're in this together."

The kids lies on his stomach behind the front seat and covers himself with newspapers. We race towards the border. A guard stops me at the border booth.

"Passport please, Ma' am."

"Miss."

I give him mine. The cover is torn, the pages yellowish and folded at the corners. The guard grimly looks through it.

"But this passport expired in 1963. How long has it been since you've been back?"

"What's it to you? I'll get a new one when I get to Los Angeles."

The booth phone rings; the guard gets distracted by it and waves me by. I step on the gas, speed three blocks. Turn right. Stop on a muddy street.

"What the hell happened, kid? Why do they hate you? Because you are with *me*?"

"No. We needed stuff and I got it," the kid says, biting into a candy bar.

"Did you steal?"

"No, I just took stuff."

"That's called stealing, damn it. That's really, really wrong. Let me see . . . what did you get?"

The kid starts taking everything from the bag. "Candy bars, chocolates, the latest issue of Cars magazine, a toothbrush, two toothbrushes, two wrinkled bills, and more candy bars."

"You also stole money?"

"No. I said you were my grandmother and you were going to die."

"Me? Your grandma? Jesus! I could never be your grandmother. How much money exactly?"

"Two five-dollar bills."

"I'm dying and they only gave you two fives? Stingy pieces of shit . . ."

I rip out the pages of my passport and start the car. As I drive, I throw them out the window as if they were scrap paper. The kid turns, sees a car behind us drive over my passport cover and keenly looks ahead again. Neither of us looks back any more. Neither of us has a passport or a reason to go back.

Silver and Gold

The impenetrable blackness of the night obscured the ocean. My feet hung off the edge of the pier. Down in the sea, floating plankton made the color of the water change—red, yellow, and even orange. I closed my eyes.

The smell of barbecue in the distance melted with the fish odor, and the buzz of an old car in the distance mingled with the waves breaking off the pier.

"Do you want stories?" Dmitri asked, "I have some stories."

Dmitri wasn't usually that open with me. He was probably drunk. A half-empty one-liter bottle of beer and Dmitri's favorite fish—yellowtail—and damp crackers lay beside us on the pier. The sky turned sable violet over the ebony sea.

"What kind of stories?" I asked, taking a sip from the bottle.

"Watch stories." He moved his bare feet in the water, making circles.

"What kinds of stories?"

"All kinds. Every one of my watches has a story." Dmitri searched in his jacket where he had all the watches he'd stolen. Silver and gold gleamed.

I separated the silver ones from the gold since I preferred the silver watches. Gold is orange-colored.

He picked a really old, wide, flat pocket watch and moved its dull golden ring. "This has a good story, a sad story."

"Wait. Hold on. I'm going to write this down." I flipped open my notebook and started writing. *It's a sad story* I wrote.

"Come on, continue." I told him.

"There were two brothers who lived in Poland during the First World War. They had a watch store, but because of the danger they decided to escape to America. The little brother traveled first to find a place to set up a new store. He moved to a small town in Paraguay. The older brother was supposed to send all the money and the watches they had. Nothing arrived, not even the brother. The little brother didn't have money, so he had to start working fixing watches. He never made enough money to go back to Poland, but from friends' letters he knew his brother had sold the store and run away with the money. He wanted revenge. Day by day, he saved money to go back, but it was never enough, and as the years passed and he had to support a family, he finally gave up the idea of going back." I wrote:

> He finally gave up the idea of going back, but he never gave up the hate. One day, when he was more than eighty years old, he received a strange box. The postman said that the box had been missing for years; that's the way the mail is in Paraguay, he said. The old Polish man shook the box and heard small pieces moving inside. The box was full of watches and a note from his brother from forty-nine years ago, saying he was taking the next ship that afternoon to meet him in Paraguay. Obviously he had died getting there. The watches were old and no longer had any value. The old man took the box to the main square of the town and left it there. Lots of kids flocked near the box, picking watches. No one wanted the damned orange-colored pocket watch.

As I finished, I looked at Dmitri's profile, wondering. So

Dmitri was also a story collector? Were we the same after all? If he was lying, he was making it up just for me. I was the only witness to his lies.

"You're weird, eh?" Dmitri muttered in a drunken voice. "Instead of enjoying the story and letting it move you, you write it. Can't you just listen?"

"Well, nothing really moves me, you know? Real feelings and people are not my main interest," I sneered, amazed I had said that to him; I had said it because I wrote so much about him I felt I had known him for years.

"I'm going into the water," he said and slipped off his sleeveless T-shirt.

"Are you nuts? It's almost eleven o' clock, and it's cold." I was afraid he might drown because he was drunk.

"You're not afraid of the water, are you?"

"Me? Of course not." I didn't let my hands tremble.

"You know how to swim, don't you?"

"Yes . . ."

"Ah, because if you don't, it'd be difficult to write about me."

As he removed his pants, I saw his shabby underwear. I swear I didn't want to see, but he stood in front of me, challenging me. So I covered my eyes with my hands. With both of them.

"What do you think you're doing?" I felt hot on the outside and the inside.

"Don't look if you don't want to," he said, pulling off his underwear. I put my hands over my face, but unconsciously spied through my fingers, spotting his white parts.

He splashed into the dark water; I lost him in the harbor and I hated that I lost him. Then his head came up, and I turned around so he wouldn't see me smile. He kept on swimming around with no style. Later he made circles and floated for a while, butt-upwards, pretending to be dead.

"Are you coming in?" he yelled, waving his hand.

"Beg your pardon?"

"Do you want to write about this?"

"Well, yes . . ."

"Then if you want to describe how it feels, you have to come in and feel it."

I worriedly looked at my dry clothes and calculated the distance and the quantity of water that separated us.

"The water is even better at night. You sure you're not afraid?"

I didn't answer this time. He floated on his back, face skyward. His intimate parts floated to the surface.

I thought over and over that I wasn't going to let him humiliate me. "Close your eyes," I yelled back, slithering out of my suit, staying in my snowy white pajamalike underwear. No way I was going to take that off.

With pure panic, I held my nose, closed my eyes tightly, and jumped into the water. It wasn't cold actually, it was freezing. My underwear filled with liquid and inflated like a hissing balloon. Sloshing, I try to imitate the impeccable crawl I had seen others do. But I think I looked like a dog. As I swam toward him, salty little waves punched my nose.

"Can I ask you a question?" Dmitri muttered.

"Sure."

"You talk so much about art; now, how come you are a writer and not a painter?"

"Because paintings are completed, and then you can't change them anymore. I hate endings.

"Screenplays have endings too."

"You can always change words. Painters live more in the present than writers. Not that I like to live in the past, but I like to remember."

"So you say that you can write the same story all your life?"

"Until it's ready."

"How do you know when it's ready?"

"I'll know it. I think I'll know."

"How long do you think it'd take you to write my story?"

"We'll see . . ."

I swam away and submerged my head, hearing the heavy underwater sound.

Suddenly the water made me anxious, so I quickly swam toward him. He was floating calmly, head half underwater, his eyes out, staring at me. I stared at him intensely, at his blue eyes, at their glow reflecting the waves of the magenta water.

"Don't you think that words have limits?" he finally asked.

"What limits?"

"Well, not everybody can read, you know."

"I hate ignorance. People who can't read will never understand my work—they'll never understand me."

"How do you know they won't understand you without reading you?"

"I know." I swam back to the pier, moving my arms and legs awkwardly.

I held tightly to the pine-tar wooden wall, staying still in the water, trying to dominate fear. From the water, I grabbed the beer bottle and took the last sip; he glanced at me and did the same. With a gesture, I made him look away until I was out of the water. When I crawled up, my wet underwear stuck to my chest. The fabric was transparent, revealing my dark zones, outlining the shape of my bones. I covered myself with my hands, crossed my legs. He turned around, opening his nostrils, and by then I knew that he made that gesture when something bothered him.

"Aren't you afraid that maybe the story of the Polish guy will happen to you?" he said fiercely, without looking at me.

"Yes, I'm a little afraid of being old, but by then I'll be a famous writer, so no one will care if I have wrinkles or not."

"I don't mean old, I mean losing too much of your time hating."

"I won't lose time."

"No?"

"No." I looked at the distorted reflection of my face in the water. I don't remember seeing the slightest expression of doubt.

Wine Violet, Purple, Grape

Sirens, horns, breaking glass, garbage trucks, loud crowds. The sounds of San Pedro port have changed. The red, Italian canteen I went to with Dmitri is now a shoe store. The pier where we fished is falling apart. The water where we swam is thick and dirty and dark. And where his boat used to be, now there is a big empty space, bigger and emptier than the moon.

"Well, things haven't changed that much," I tell the kid, so he doesn't get discouraged. Evidently, someone destroyed it all. I don't know exactly who, but I know why. Americans want to destroy my story so I can't tell it.

I stop at a newspaper stand and buy a *Variety*. On the cover there's an article about women writers in Hollywood. A Writers Guild of America survey shows only twenty percent of working writers are women.

"We're still a minority in Hollywood. See, kid? Things haven't changed that much."

Rainbow-colored oil stains and trash drift in the water. There are video stores, coffee shops, Japanese tourists, modern cars, signs in Spanish, but things haven't changed that much.

With some confusion, I stop at a coffee shop where two guys with baseball caps drink smoothies. "See, kid. Across this street was the bar where I met him. I swear, damn it."

"How can you be so sure. Your memory is not exactly great."

"Look, even though I don't remember some things, unfortunately I can remember others more than I'd care to."

The kid and I sit on a rotten bench where some dark green moss grows. The kid pouts; I know what he wants.

"Would you stop thinking about food? Food can kill you just like experience can." The kid stares at me angrily.

"Okay, I'll tell you about me a little more so you'll be distracted. I'll tell you about me and food." When you tell stories to kids they become hypnotized, and freezing the thinking process is the only way to make them forget disdain.

"While we find a pay phone, I'll tell you about food, follow me." I pull his arm and drag him down the street. When you tell stories to kids, they will also follow you anywhere.

"My mother lived to cook, so I was supposed to live to eat, but I didn't. My mother was an awkward thief. She wasn't a big one, she just selected things she wanted from other people's houses and took them. Small things like napkins and salt shakers. She especially loved embroidered handkerchiefs."

The kid looks at me, incredulous. We turn at the corner.

"She used to be a professional violinist with the Rome Philharmonic. She had the soft skin of a fat woman; lots of long, red hair; and dark, gloomy eyes, eyes deep and dark like basements. Her eccentricity was that she always dressed in violet—dark violet, purple violet, grape—and she drank only red wine. She just loved violet."

"Did she also care about colors, like you?" The kid asks. "Not as much as food. To her, if you were fat it meant you were healthy, so I looked very sick to her. We never talked much, so I never told her what I did to my father."

"What did you do to him?"

"It's a long story."

"You're making this whole story up so I won't ask about food, aren't you?"

"No, not at all. Mom gave up her career and beauty to stay home for my father. She became heavy and quiet with him, like an anchor is to a boat. And when Pa died, she started sinking like the city of Venice. Seeing her, I realized what I didn't want from life. Loving too much can make you brush the boundaries of insanity."

"But you love Dmitri, right? Otherwise, why come all the way here?"

"Love him? Ha! Not at all. On the contrary. I hate him. I really, really hate him."

The kid stops, figures something out and stares at me. "Dmitri doesn't exist, does he?"

I don't answer and keep walking, looking down at the pavement.

He jumps in front of me. "I'm right! You made him up."

"I only made up part of it."

When we get to the phone booth, I grab the phone book, but I can't find Dmitri's number because I don't know his last name. Did I ever know it?

Not even the directory assistance operator knows where to find a guy with that name and no last name, or maybe she doesn't want to tell me.

We sit on a truck for a moment, letting the sun hit us,

and my aching bones tell me that coming here wasn't such a good idea after all. The proof is that not even the thin trees protect me from the orange-colored sun.

"They're after me, kid."

"Who?"

"All the Americans. Everybody. Everybody who feels. They hate me because I managed not to feel."

So I decide to wander around, questioning strange people. Some don't even respond, others shake their heads. Half an hour later, I collapse on a bench, looking for answers in the shoes passing by. Discouraged, the kid sits next to me.

As my time slips away from me, I watch a taxi stop at the corner. Relaxing in his seat, the driver drinks from a can of beer. He has a shitty car, but it has a TV to watch soap operas, and of course he has money for alcohol.

Alcohol. Bars. Of course: bars. After all, that's where I found him. "Look for bars, kid. Dmitri liked to drink beer."

Suddenly high, I drag the kid to several bars. "Do you know a guy called Dmitri?" All I get back is "No, No." At a table outside of a modest, seedy bar, four drunk men chat and drink Tecate beer. They laugh when I mention the name and whisper among themselves secretly. Devastated and dragging my feet across the street, I suddenly see the bar where I met him. It was there all along, after all. Only it was on a different street from where I thought it was.

"It's not that I didn't remember where it was, kid. I just forgot. It could happen to anyone."

And then and there I see an old, gray-haired bartender with a tattoo on his arm. A lighthouse tattoo. It's the same bartender who worked in the bar when I met Dmitri. Only he is much older and with duller eyes.

"Hi . . ." I mumble, "I don't know if you remember me. I was here a few years ago . . . only a couple of years ago actually, and . . . do you happen to know the name of a fisherman called Dmitri? The one who stole watches."

The bartender laughs a drunken laugh, holding his belly. "The watch thief? His name is Joe."

"What do you mean his name is Joe? Did he change his name?"

"I think he was always called that." Maybe he changed his name so no one would find him.

"Where can I find him?"

"Ever been to East LA?

The bartender writes down a telephone number on a paper napkin.

Gathering my strength in my legs, I run to the phone as if it were an oasis in the middle of the desert of my life.

"That means he exists?" the kid yells, following me.

"Not only that . . ." I say, "That means he's alive."

Trembling, I dash with all the energy of my rusty, long-disused hope. Once on the phone again, while I dial nervously and out of breath, I think of what the hell I'm going to say. I don't know if I should salute him or curse him. It rings long rings, once, twice . . . It takes eight agonizing rings until someone picks up. Then a woman's voice answers, "*¿Hola? ¿Hola?*" Confused, I hang up roughly. Who could it be? He didn't have a mother or sisters.

It's better this way; it's better if I don't tell him anything until I see his face. A visit would be just fine.

We get in the car which rumbles as I start it. The kid stares at me, waiting. From his wide eyes, I can tell he is still hungry.

"You know, kid, you don't need food just like I never needed Dmitri. If you can stop your impulses, you will never go crazy. You know what? My aunts said I was going to be crazy just like my mother. What a silly thing to say, don't you think? I'm perfectly normal," I say, cleaning out the glove compartment where I hid the gun in a purple handkerchief embroidered with violet motifs.

Ice Blue

I think it was a dull lilac, fall Monday, or maybe it was a wild-berry-red Friday; I'm not sure of the exact date. How could I be? It was almost fifty years ago.

At the network studio that day, I was arranging my things on the desk, and before sitting down, I realized that Barbara's desk was empty. Markins walked by, not looking at me.

"Where's Barbara?" I said.

"She left." A long silence followed. Markins crumpled a piece of paper and threw it in the trash.

"Why?"

"She didn't want to talk, so she had to."

I was confused, a mix between nervous and sad.

"Where's she working?"

"Working?" He laughed out loud.

"Where is she, then?"

"I dunno. The lucky ones go to Europe. But most like her go to Canada or Mexico."

Markins exited, and I was left to my thoughts. "Mexico?"

That night when I got home, Pa was watching television, drinking a screwdriver. The news on TV showed images of McCarthy and then images of Korea, while a reporter announced that the war was over. Angrily I turned the damn thing off.

"What the heck are you doing? You like the news. Did

you know Lucy was subpoenaed? But she's okay. I knew she wasn't a Red. I love Lucy. Hee-hee."

"Someone blacklisted my friend Barbara. Do you know who?"

He stood up, went to the bar, squeezed an orange, and poured the juice in his glass. He drank a long sip of his drink before answering. "You know it's not my fault if they're anti-patriots, you know? We're in a war, damn it. The only way to survive is to kill first." He turned the TV on again and changed the dial. Gene Kelly danced smoothly.

"You questioned her knowing she was my friend?"

"I wouldn't have done it if it hadn't been absolutely necessary. Don't worry, there was no need to use psychological tricks. She admitted her guilt right away."

I turned off the television, furious. Pa grabbed my hand firmly and glared at me. Knowing my nerves, I let go of his gasp. "You're a son-of-a-bitch, Daddy."

Pa got enraged and slapped me. I think I fell on the floor then. He took a wooden hanger and hit me with it. When I lifted my head, I saw his orange drink right in front of me, so I avoided looking at it. From the floor, I counted colors like I always did, as the wooden hanger fell over and over on my back. Bleach blue, dark blue, baby blue . . .

This wasn't the first time. Sometimes he got mad at me, but I never understood why. And when the poor guy got mad, he had no option but to punish me. Generally he used a wooden hanger, so it wouldn't be his hand that hit me. There was also the sink treatment—if she cries uncontrollably, submerge the head of the girl underwater until the girl swallows so much water she almost drowns and has to stop crying. Infallible. Consequences might include that the girl will have a fear of water, but it's guaranteed that she will stop crying for the rest of her life.

When he punished me, I would play dead, focusing my eyes on the colors of objects without really seeing, concentrating on counting and counting. Little by little, my skin would become rough, and I wouldn't feel anymore.

That same night I went to the network when everyone was gone and typed frantically at my typewriter. I wrote an article with my own list with names. I titled it "Black List of Rats."

As I took the paper out of the typewriter and looked at it, I felt scared. Then I tore it into tiny pieces. Maybe a tear rolled down my cheek.

Afterwards, I passed through a kind of writer's block, wrote stupid things, tore it all up and started again, and again, and again. Frustrated, I sat at my desk for hours, looking at the blank page of a notebook. Nothing came. Then I tried to write on the floor. Nothing. Then I tore the pages out in a very bad mood, quickly moved to the bed, sat on top of the pillows, lay upside-down. Not one word.

Finally, I stood, posing in front of a mirror and frowning at my image. Whenever I started a phrase that didn't have the exact tone I wanted, I got so grumpy that I had to cover all the mirrors with scarves, so I wouldn't see my face.

I didn't know what tone I wanted for my screenplay. I started with a cherry-romantic tone, then it changed into an ironic turquoise, to end up in a flat, dull malt. The tone had to be Dmitri's, so I held on tightly to my notebook and strode to the marina.

The ocean throbbed against the severe wind, and the white, foamy waves crashed into the gray granite jetty. The olive green hull of a ship, two jade bottles, a flag with a strip of green. I didn't think there was such a thing as writer's block, but I thought there was such a thing as writer's squint. Believing I had to be with Dmitri all day long to catch the timbre of his voice, I asked him:

"I can pay you if you let me stay on your boat from today on. Anyway, in three days, you'll be gone." At the time I thought I only did it so I could write about him, not so I could stay with him.

"No," he growled. What would your family say?"

"I don't care. I plan to get out of that damned house anyway. Travel. I'm like you."

"I'm not like that."

"What about staying just for tonight? It may rain," I pouted, making my best little-girl eyes.

He said no. He said he had only one bed. He said that beds on boats are called berths. He said that he liked to be alone.

I looked anxiously at the small berth in the forward cabin. It was about three feet wide—not enough space for two people—so I moved my eyes to him. To my surprise, he was staring right at my skinny, unshapely body, smiling.

"What?" I asked.

"Nothing," he mumbled, walking to the oven. I watched him walk. His antique beige pajamas showed his hairy, muscular legs.

I wrote: *The truth is I don't want you around. I'd rather be alone, but I like your bony body.*

I would have liked him to think this, but he kept fixing the wrinkled sheets on his bed. I could never figure out what he thought.

He took a fried yellowtail and tomato sandwich from the small compartment beside the oven and shared it with me. I sat at the table; he sat beside me. The wind blew, the ocean snorted, and it looked as if the sky wanted to cry.

"Who are you escaping from?" I asked him.

"I can't tell you."

"Then I'm right, you're escaping from someone."

He lowered his eyes.

"Are you afraid of being thrown in jail?"

"I was already in jail. Twice. Once for helping a friend. The other for helping myself."

"I knew you weren't afraid. Just like I described you. If you aren't afraid of going to jail, why are you leaving?"

"I was subpoenaed again. I'm afraid of those FBI bastards. I'm tired of fighting. I want to look for new places, new seas, new watches, especially for one watch."

"I thought you weren't afraid . . ."

"It's difficult to be a hero when you don't want to lose your work or go crazy."

"But if you dodge the subpoena, you won't be able to come back or work in the U.S. for who knows how long. You'd be free in other countries, but not in your own."

He muttered something, but because of his accent, I

couldn't understand it.

I wrote: *What use is it belonging to a country if my mouth can't belong to my ideas?*

He said: "You're right. It's sad. After all, this is a shitty country, but it's mine."

I was wrong about him one more time. So I was about to cross out the words but decided not to. Maybe he was wrong about himself. After all, I could see things in him he didn't see.

After we finished the sandwich, I didn't know what to do with my hands so I sat on one of them. He and his boat made me feel unstable. I got dizzy with all the ups and downs of the waves and regretted immediately having eaten the sandwich. The fish began to climb up my throat, but I swallowed it; I didn't want him to know I wasn't brave enough. To change the subject, I gave him a piece of my prose. He looked at it; I stared at his blue eyes sweeping over the page.

> Mexico has a lot to give you and nothing. It's a country built on sand dreams, constantly afraid of being blown away. A country that lives thinking about future possibilities. A country that doesn't reason, that—like a baby— only moves by sensation. A country that likes to show its red lights, musical soul, and summer mood, but underneath it runs a black river full of God-knows-what rancor. A river where a person was buried alive, and whose ghost struggles underneath the country. A dead country that only thinks that it's alive because of an assemblage of blurred events when the country was young, when she didn't know about disappointments, about blue afternoons. Read again, I am Mexico.

Then he glanced at me, silent.

"Do you like it?"

"Yeah," he mumbled.

"By reading it, now you know more about me."

"Okay."

"Did you notice it has a lot of death images?"

He shook his head. From the hint of emotion he showed, I understood he hated them. I didn't lose hope, though, and looked at him intrigued, "Have you ever been near . . . death, I mean?"

"Many times, I guess. I never counted them."

"Really?" I smiled. Death was my favorite subject, even though the only person I had actually seen dying was my father. Usually I would plan my own. A spectacular death, something that would appear in the newspapers with big pictures: young lady jumps from the Empire State Building. Something really bloody and bizarre: young lady jumps from the Empire State with a letter in her hand, but she covers the page and no one will ever know her last words. Something like that, an original, red death. I don't like blue deaths—asphyxia, drowning or other blue deaths of that sort. I was going to plan it very carefully, even the color of my dress. Pink is a good color to die in. However, I hoped I wouldn't lie in a bad position, or with my mouth open—I wouldn't mind being dead if I looked beautiful. I wanted to look dead but pretty.

"What I don't want is to die in a stupid way," I said. "Get a massive concussion from slipping in the bathtub, for example, or get electrocuted by a kitchen appliance. A toaster," I smirked, seeing the awful image.

"Poisoned by bad milk that costs eighteen cents in the market." He smiled with his gap teeth, and we began to laugh. His laugh was like hiccups—catching. When I stretched my legs, I lightly touched his bare knees under the table. All of a sudden, I got serious.

"I worry about people."

"When one dies, people forget. At any funeral, if you were a son of a bitch, people forget that."

"When we talk about death, you think about after you are dead; I think about before it, the last minutes before I'm dead, if someone is going to be there when I'm dying. I don't want to be alone."

"I'll try to be there." I briefly held his hand.

"Do you really want to know what I think about you?" he said.

"I don't care," Even though I really wanted to know, I glanced at my short nails. I wondered if I looked disheveled, and I passed my hand through my hair. "Okay. Tell me . . ."

"You think too much," he said, tore a piece of paper out of my notebook, and started chewing it.

I couldn't believe it, but I acted like it was nothing.

"Too much thinking . . ." he repeated.

"Don't you think before you do things?"

"I just do."

The sea scrambled. The waves struggled. I think.

"I plan my life because I don't want to make mistakes. It's not wrong. I've written down the titles of my next twenty-three screenplays. And you? What do you want to do with your life?"

"How can I possibly know yet?" He swallowed the paper. "I don't know, I'll tell you when I'm ninety-six."

I didn't smile. "I mean, aren't you planning to settle down . . . love someone enough to maybe . . . stop stealing and traveling . . . not that you have to . . . just a thought?"

"I'm looking for an hour-glass clock. That's why I've traveled so much. I've looked for it from the Antarctic to Finland. Maybe when I find it, I'll settle down."

I wondered why he wanted an hour-glass clock. He paused again, and I wrote: *With it, I could control time. When I want, I'd turn it, and the sand would run with time. If I want time to stop, I just won't move it.*

"What are you thinking?" I asked.

"Nothing."

"Why don't you keep talking?"

"I only speak when I have something to say," he grumbled.

Then he stared at me really hard, as if he were practicing telepathy or something. I tried to return his stare, but I couldn't; my eyes wandered to the cabin wall behind his head, searching for another color white to add in my mind.

Outside, a fluorescent yellow lightning struck, cracking the cobalt sky. Somebody felt lewd and hollow, but I don't remember it being me. I just flinched.

"Told you, you're strange. But in a good way," he said. "All right, all right, you can sleep over, but only for tonight, eh?"

I embraced him to thank him and got too close, and he gently pushed me away. He opened the palm of his hand and I thought he was offering to lead me to his bed, but he rubbed his fingers, meaning he wanted money. Politely I gave him some.

He offered me the right side of the bed, so I could sleep facing south. "That's what you like, isn't it?"

"You remembered."

The sheets smelled of lemon. I wonder if it was a French essence he might have bought in Paris or just lemon juice.

I watched him bending over the bed. Without looking at him, I curled up and lay on the edge of the bed reading a book. I peeked over the edge of my book to see what he was doing. He was flipping through a magazine. His stomach showed the rhythm of his breathing. When he glanced at me, I hid behind the book.

"Ready to sleep?"

"Yes."

"Good night, then."

"Good night."

He turned off the lantern.

What do you mean by turning the light off? I sleep with the light on! I wanted to squeak, but I didn't and stared at the wall as the boat rocked. Afraid that any part of his body might touch mine, I closed my eyes tight and started counting colors in my head: chocolate brown, powder blue, fly green, cherry, terra-cotta. Brown won. When a color wins, it has the power.

Then I opened my eyes in the dark. After a while, I started seeing in the moonlight. He moved a lot while he slept and made weird facial expressions. A nervous tic under his eyes and a grimace around his mouth. Even his breath was odd: too fast. Obviously something was bothering him. I wondered what he was dreaming about. I wondered if he was dreaming about me.

Starting to feel caged, I opened the hatch. A lighthouse beam shone in and made an ochre drawing on his tan check. Confused, I lay on the mattress and sank there like an anchor. I felt at the center of a volcano, so hot and so lost. His eyes moved fast under his eyelids, and then his windburned lips turned into a broad smile. He hummed something I couldn't understand. I watched him, wanting to decipher what he was mumbling. So I moved my eyes closer to his mouth. His lips moved so slowly I couldn't comprehend. Suddenly he rolled over, and his arm almost hit me.

Finally, I flipped around, lying head to toe on the mattress, away from him, on the edge of the bed. Because there was only one pillow, and it was under his head, I put my face over his cushioned calf.

Falling asleep, I thought about the dark bottom of the sea. No light penetrates below one thousand meters. The clearer the water, the deeper the light penetrates. I thought that if I were water I would be black.

"Kid, why don't you roll down the window, so you can see?"
The soil is black here like raw onyx.

He doesn't obey me. With the windows covered with
dust, the kid and I arrive at the East LA address. It is an old,
awful house in the slums—pale cement over bricks and
rusted, sheet-metal roof. A tomato plantation behind it. The
tomatoes aren't ripe, so their color is faded, making them
look orange from here. Even if the walls of the house are the
same color, I won't allow myself to count it. The soil around
the house is dry and cracked. It doesn't seem like it could be
his home. It's far away from Dmitri's eternal, ethereal ocean.

We decide to wait in the car until he comes out of the
house. The kid rolls down the window only an inch, and we
stay there hiding, our faces down, just our foreheads showing.

"Are you sure you'll be able to recognize him if he walks
out? I mean, after so many years . . . he might be changed."

"Just open the damned window, will you?" I just hate
summer, but I don't run the air conditioner because it over-
heats the engine. I bet the kid doesn't like this car, but I've
had it for eighteen years already. At least it is a loyal car. We
stay spying like this for almost one hour, sharing a can of
coke and some chocolate, which I let him finish.

A few hours later, I wake up startled by a noise; I notice
that the sleeping head of the kid is on my lap. A big-breasted,
overweight woman in her fifties has appeared with a sleeping

baby on her shoulder. She walks out to pick a tomato from the field. As she walks, three children follow her, clinging to her legs. One is about ten, has curly, blond hair, and wears a pirate eye-patch; the other two are twins of about four and have their bangs trimmed too short.

I immediately get out of the car because I have to know more—maybe Dmitri is inside. As I walk toward the woman, the kid follows me, hiding behind my dress. As I get closer, I notice the woman is wearing an tawdry, tight, pink dress and a dirty caramel apron. She has a mustache and smiles at me. She doesn't even know me, but she smiles.

"Hello," I snicker, "Nice to meet you."

"*Hola,*" she approaches, "*No hablo inglés.*"

Oh dear! The last thing I expected to happen—I don't remember Dmitri speaking Spanish, but of course after all these years, perhaps he had learned. I know Castilian Spanish, the original language people speak in Spain. I know a bit of Mexican Spanish, but I refuse to speak in that language, as I refused to speak my mother's Southern Italian. As with everything else in my life, I like only pure things, not deformations.

"*Mi nombre es Carla Arnone.*" If Dmitri mentioned me, it's possible she knows who I am.

She looks at me dumbfounded. She has never heard my name and has no idea who I am. Oh, well, maybe she is not important enough for him to mention me.

"Dmitri?" I ask.

"Joe? *Cuando* young, Dmitri, now Joe."

"Okay. Joe."

"No here." She curves her thick mouth. "No here . . ." she opens her hand showing me ten fingers, "*diez* years, no here." She separates the kids from herself.

Making an effort to curve my tongue to pronounce like she does, I ask, "*¿Dónde?* Where?"

The woman shakes her head; she doesn't know. If she doesn't know, who will know? The kid is jumping in the yard, playing with one of the children who looks his own age, holding hands under a fig tree.

The woman yells at them in Spanish to calm them down. "*Quietos, niñitos, si no, su abuela se va a enojar.*"

Spanish is such a feminine language—long complicated paragraphs full of weird adjectives and adverbs. It's a language too passionate for me. English is simple and strict—like men. I'd rather speak in English, clear messages, short sentences, no double meanings, no lies. You almost can't lie in English. The three children don't listen to the woman and keep on playing.

"Joe's *nietos*," she exclaims pointing to the children.

Of course, I know that *nietos* means grandchildren, but I act as if I don't understand. So he had a family. How sweet of her to take care of the grandchildren of others. The woman is not disappointed at my silence. She invites me into the house. She is too friendly, or maybe she wants something from me . . . she doesn't fool me for a second.

Inside everything is messy, plastic toys everywhere and some of the walls have paint and kids' pen marks. The place is full of plants and has a muddy floor. The woman offers me a chair. I sit, staring at the scars on her feet, which look like they were pecked by chickens. She is much younger than I, but she looks like shit. Overweight, overtired, overhappy, a complete shame. She offers me coffee and bread. She doesn't have butter she says, only coffee and plain bread which she offers for dipping. Maybe she's trying to be nice to me so I will tell her about my relationship with Dmitri. And why not? I am about to tell her everything about us, when I see her wedding ring, so I answer, "No coffee, thank you."

On the dinner table are several photos—pictures of the children and grandchildren of different ages. I flip through quickly. One photo is Dmitri and a woman getting married, both in white—he is tan and his smile shows the gap in his teeth, and he looks a few years older than when I met him, maybe just three years older. Then I see a faded photo of Dmitri at the pier; same haircut as the wedding, probably same year. He grins, holding in his hand an hour-glass clock.

I wasn't there when he found it. That fat bitch was. I look at her; her face is all sweaty. Squinting, I want to ask her if she hated him sometimes and how much exactly. I bet she didn't; she couldn't possibly as much as I did. Without saying a thing, I look around. The kid and her grandsons are yelling, the baby screaming.

"*Adios*," I tell her out of the blue.

"*¡Adios!*" She waves her hand.

I grab the kid's arm and drag him to the car without being able to take my eye off her. She embraces the kids; they hang from her arms and back. She maternally strokes their heads and stares at me as if she wants to say something. I glare back.

"*¿Que?*" I ask, grabbing the kid's arm.

"*La iglesia.*"

"The church?" I repeat. "What about it? You think he could be there? *¿El está ahí?*"

"*Quizás.*"

She's not sure, but it's the only clue I have, so I am going to hold on to it. As I arrange my hair, I scurry fast to the car, dragging the kid along. We get in and drive farther south. I don't look back, only south. My past is south. My lost past.

On the road, I feel as if I forgot something in the house. I begin to hate a brown stain I see on the dash. I was expecting Dmitri to wait for me. Not that I care. But he even had grandkids. While holding the wheel with my left hand, I rub the brown stain with my right index finger. I can't stand that stain.

"Why didn't you marry?" the kid asks, rubbing his nose on the sleeve of his shirt.

"How did you know I wasn't . . ."

"You thought out loud again."

"Can you believe the son-of-a-bitch got married?"

The kid shrugs, cleaning the dirt from his fingernails. "Well, what did ya expect? In fifty years, I'm gonna marry at least four times." He always exaggerates.

I don't know why I'm not married or at least involved, or why I never found a decent boyfriend. I don't know why I'm here, searching for a person I don't even know. "There's nothing wrong with being single, you know."

The kid arranges the tapes in the glove compartment.

"Maybe this is a stupid question," I begin, "but why in

the name of God is life so hard?" I ask him, a ten-year-old kid.

He rolls his eyes and says, "You?"

"What do you mean by *you*?"

"I mean, I've been in the streets a lot and heard people's problems, but your life is more difficult than any other life I've ever heard. It's not that I've heard about too many lives in ten years, but yours seems kind of the worst somehow."

"Maybe you're right. Maybe it's a little bit my fault. But only a little, eh?" I don't know why, but I have the sensation that I forgot something in the house, that I've lost something.

As I scoff twice, I pity the woman in the house, but at the same time, I don't give a damn. Poor woman, trapped all her life with those children, has no life of her own while I feel independent. She seemed happy, though.

"Let's go to the church!" I push the accelerator. The woman didn't tell me what church, but I know exactly where to go. After all these years, he hasn't changed.

I cough, choking, and spit a blood spot on the handkerchief, which I hide from the kid. Insecure, I search inside my purse again to make sure I didn't forget something in the house. I don't know what it could be; I didn't have anything to lose that wasn't lost already.

When I left the network alone that magenta night, two FBI agents in dirty brown stopped me, showing their shiny badges.

"Federal Bureau of Investigation, Ma' am." One handed me a letter. As I read it, my eyes grew big.

"Subpoena? Me? Why? I didn't do anything. I'm not one of them."

But they wouldn't listen to any of my yelling and complaining. One just pointed at the letterhead.

"You're expected at that address tomorrow."

"Wait a minute. Who named me?"

Silent, they walked to a black Cadillac parked at the curb. I followed them, hiding behind a studio stage. It wasn't so dark that I couldn't see that my father was in that car.

Later that day, scared, I waited outside Dmitri's boat. When I saw him come out, I followed him, because I was convinced he also had hidden things from me.

He ended up in a small church, more like a chapel—tiny, white, wooden house topped with a cross in the middle— outside town in a grove of skinny trees. I walked close behind him, trying not to make noise with my heels, hiding beneath a man's hat. But when he opened the door to the chapel and turned around, he saw me behind him and stopped me.

"Did you follow me here?" he asked.

"Me? No, not at all." I forced a smile, "I was just going to church. I didn't know you went to church."

I froze in silence outside the door, asking God to convince him I wasn't lying. The only other times I remember talking with God were to ask him for things: presents, books, deaths.

"So . . . what time is it in Poland now?" I asked, nervous. He took out his old flat gold watch, and he was going to tell me, but he gazed at me instead and said, smiling, "You don't really want to know, do you?"

He grinned broadly and stared at me with his blackish blue eyes. I never knew what to say when he looked at me so interestingly yet disturbingly. A navy blue car drove around the corner. Two FBI agents in brown suits and hats looked at me, and I wondered if they had followed me while I was following him. Dmitri saw them and gestured to me to go in. To me, church meant lies, so I didn't want my character to go to church. That was not what I had planned for him.

"I don't think you really want to go in there," I said.

"Why not?"

"Because you aren't afraid of anything."

"Sometimes I feel you've got me confused with somebody else. The guy in your little book maybe," he smiled, revealing the pink gap in his teeth, "I like it here because you can sit and remember."

Remember, huh? I searched for a memory. The dreadful face of my father. A sad sensation of hollowness invaded me. "It's strange, I can't remember anything. Can you?"

"Would you stop with the damned questions. Shall we go in?"

"Sure."

Inside, the chapel was full of ivory, marble sculptures of

the Virgin and saints I didn't know, and I wondered if they were the same in all countries. A big medieval painting of a dying angel was hanging to one side. Two huge, stained-glass windows were on the other side; their light brightened the haze of incense. Squinting, I blocked the brightness of the light with my hand.

"Follow me," he whispered and walked toward the apse. "I want to show you something." He headed to the confessionals, dragging me along as four women prayed, scattered in different pews. We hid behind a column, peeking at the confessionals.

A young man holding a folder came out of confession, nervously scanning the place. Confirming that no one was looking for him, he knelt down and prayed.

Then an old priest exited the confessional, went to the end of the church, and whispered to the two FBI agents in brown suits and hats who were hiding behind a fake-marble fountain.

The agents approached the young man and arrested him. He protested and tried to escape—no luck. As he struggled, pamphlets fell out of his folder. One agent picked them up and showed the other that they were "Pro Hollywood Ten" pamphlets.

When one of the agents glanced at us, we quickly turned around. As the agents carried the young man out, Dmitri glared at the confessional, whispering to me, "The sacred trust of confession doesn't exist in this country."

"How did you know what was going to happen?"

"I was also arrested here. It happens every week or so.

Priests and agents and rats are the same thing."

"Why don't you report them? Make a list of rats."

"And show it to whom? I don't have the power."

"Well, if you don't do it, then who?"

Dmitri took my hand, pulling me to the altar. As a few of the women prayed, I hoped he wouldn't go too much farther. What if somebody saw us here? I wasn't Catholic, I wasn't even Protestant. What if someone thought we were lovers? I wasn't going to let him ruin my reputation. He walked nearly all the way to the altar and knelt on one of the first pews. I sat quietly beside him on the bench and noticed that a crying mother and her bored daughter sat in front of us.

A young priest sang, and some repeated after him; I murmured, trying to follow the words, but obviously I had no idea what I was saying.

The young priest concluded, "May peace be with you . . ."

As the followers embraced, I turned to hug Dmitri, but he was hugging the crying lady and her daughter. Then I saw how he carefully slid the lady's watch from her wrist while faking being sad. When he turned to hug me, I backed up. Winking, he shrugged.

"I'm glad you believe in God," he said.

"Me too," I said, wondering if I would go to hell for lying in a holy place. I had killed what little of God was inside me a long time ago.

"You know, when I was a kid I wanted to be a priest, but the attraction of the sea was stronger."

A priest? I imagined Dmitri in a black robe; his face framed by black fabric, he would look like a mountain. No way I was going to put this in my screenplay. Once my notes were finished, I would erase things from his life and create a better reality for him.

"I like the brick walls here," he muttered. "Not like those fake-wood walls. These are *real* bricks, solid, did you notice?"

"I like what's on the walls. The medieval frescoes."

"You mean the windows?" he pointed to the stained glass. "Those are nice windows. Huge. You can see through the colors."

"Shhhh," a woman in a carmine hat hissed from the back.

Then we shut up, so I couldn't explain that frescoes were paintings, but I supposed it didn't matter, because I felt like he wasn't there with me any more. In a mysterious peace, he joined his knees and feet, held his palms together, smiled at me, and lowered his head.

Feeling out of place, I glanced around at the gold-colored saints' halos in the paintings. *A dull gold, a mix of golds, a static, queenly gold. I lost track of how to describe the color; some things can't be caged in words.*

Perhaps the real Dmitri would know. "How would you describe the color of the halos?" I asked.

"They're just yellow."

He slowly closed his eyes; he wasn't even there—he was somewhere in his head. I wanted to bring him back from wherever he was. "How do you pray?"

"Just stop thinking."

"I can't stop thinking."

"Just stay put and stop your mind."

I sat in silence trying to stop thinking, but all I could do was remember all the details I would write later. He leaned his head on his hands, his eyes still closed, so quiet. Because I wanted to interrupt him again, I moved down the pew, making noise on purpose. Then I clenched my fingers, but he didn't even notice me.

I would have given a million pennies for his thoughts, but I knew he wouldn't accept my money for his secrets. Then I wondered if he was asking God for forgiveness. After all, God's job is to forgive.

"Stop making noise. Ask God for something. There must be something you want."

So I thought if there was something I could ask for, and I asked in my mind, I asked in silence . . . Dear God, would you kill my father?

As I kept on staring at him, he lifted his head, but kept his eyes closed. So I glanced around and decided to hold my hands tightly together, maybe I envied him. I watched what he did and tried to imitate each of his movements, because I wanted to feel what he was feeling. He smiled so beautifully that the gap between his teeth didn't matter.

I went back to the studio later that night—deserted. Again I began typing fanatically, recreating the article that had a long list of names of my father's friends, with his name included. I decided to keep the original title: "Black List of Rats."

When I finished, I took the page out of the machine looking at it proudly. Then I made handwritten copies, lots of copies, smiling like an freed woman.

Shiny Black

"Shit!" I grumble.

"Shit," the kid echoes.

Dark brown smoke comes out from under the hood, tinting the evening sky sepia. I know, I know, I forgot to put oil in the motor four years ago, but everybody makes mistakes.

I can't breathe; not even dust is blown by the lazy wind. A twenty-four-hour, red neon sign blinks on and off atop a social club. I'm sure people play cards and dice there, laughing; however, no one is inside now. Very strange. More and more I'm certain that all this is a conspiracy of happy people against me. So what if I'm not one of them? I focus on a garbage can full of stinky, rotten watermelons. This country is not how I left it. This road used to be clean. I guess nothing stays the same; even my decayed skin and restless anger change with time.

"Well, I knew we couldn't get through to my restless past," I whine. Before, I had the theory that my future was here because Dmitri was here. When I thought about my future, it gleamed, but now it fades like dust in water.

I wince at the kid as he eats chocolate and smacks his lips noisily. Unconsciously, I scowl. I've promised myself he wouldn't see me upset, because I hate it when people see my feelings.

Still chewing, the kid points toward the bar. "Do you like that car?" I don't even look to where he points; I'm looking at my shoes. He stares at my broken car, talking to it. "*Hasta la vista,* baby."

"I don't understand your generation's jokes."

"It's not a joke. This car is *gone.* I can get any car."

"But there's no car around." I walk from one side of the car to the other, trying not to look at the kid. I don't want him to see me. I feel dizzy. My memory spins. Why am I even here? I glance at my watch, as if it matters what time it is. . . .

"Get in the car, kid."

"But it's broken."

"Broken. Oh, yes, of course, I remember. I was just seeing if you remembered."

Oh, now I remember that I forgot to put oil in my car, and I'm stuck here. Whenever I get upset, I forget days and names and reasons. I lean my suddenly-heavy hip on the car.

"There's a cool car parked over there," the kid says, pointing at a car outside a funeral home. "I can steal it. I did it before. Remember, at the hospital?"

"Yeah. I remember. I remember everything." What the hell happened there? "But can we steal some poor soul's car and leave him on foot? On second thought . . . which car?"

He points. The car is an old, shiny, black hearse with curtains and a long back.

"That's a hearse for coffins, kid."

"What's a coffin?" he asks me, his mouth full of chocolate.

"It's a box, kid. You know, a box like the one they wrap Christmas presents in, but bigger. People are put inside; you know, dead people."

I sense that we are going to die here, so I take three white painkillers and try to slow down as they hit my brain. My life is fading day by day, painkiller by painkiller. I take the pills to slow down my brain; my mind works too fast, too much. I again see my wrinkles in the sideview mirror and follow one with my finger to its source near my hair. I don't want to see. I don't want to see *me*. Seeing hurts.

"How did you spend your Christmas Eve?" the kid asks me.

"What's that got to do with anything? It's none of your business."

The little veins in his forehead pop out as he turns his eyes away.

Meanwhile, I remember the Santa Claus Lane Parades on Hollywood Boulevard in the early fifties. Now *that* was Christmas. Before I went south I spent my last Christmas and New Year's all by myself in an old restaurant on Sunset at a round table set for four. I counted down the last ten seconds before midnight, but I counted them in silence. Why do people get so excited about counting? There's really no good reason to celebrate getting older and grumpier.

Coughing, I glance at the kid. Whenever I cough, the kid doesn't look at me. I keep calling him "the kid" even though that's not his real name, because I would forget his name anyway.

I cough again. Cough, cough.

I wonder for how many seconds or minutes I'm going to cough.

My throat tickles.

I'm not sick. I can control this.

I keep coughing.

My chest bumps on its own.

My back shakes with more coughing.

I taste blood.

The kid lifts my arms, although I resist.

I stop coughing.

"Thank you," I take his hands off of me and turn around.

"I'll be back," the kid beams. I see the back of his black hair moving toward the hearse.

I open the hood of my car. From the engine brown smoke burns, bubbling. I try to touch one round piece, but I have no idea what I'm doing. A fuzzy, hot stem spits at me and hisses. Better stay out of this dead engine.

I'm getting dizzier. The ground flips and the houses move closer and farther, as if they were on top of waves. Peeking at my watch, I think about what the doctor told me. "Try not to get stressed, we don't want you to lose too much weight." People pay to lose weight; I personally recommend cancer. With a little cancer losing a couple of pounds is more or less guaranteed. I've lost more weight. In fact, I lose it every day. Many women surely would envy me. I look at my bony knees peeking out my dress. Well, perhaps not that many.

As I search in the trunk of my car for food, I find a paper bag under the spare tire. I don't remember putting it there, but I open it. Inside the bag, there is a yellowing notebook with damaged corners; a dry, old pen; and three thousand dollars in twenty-dollar bills. My hands shake. Now I remember . . . I put it there just in case; it's the money my mother left me, all my savings. *Hey, kid, we're rich!* I want to yell but I don't see him, so I shrug. We're rich, but we can't move from here. I don't open my mouth. I put the gun in the paper bag and clutch it in the loneliness of the night.

Suddenly I hear the engine of the hearse roaring beside me. The kid is at the wheel; he slides over and I get in.

"What are you doing?" I yell.

"Don't shout. We're stealing it; you're supposed to be quiet."

"Sorry," I mutter, "I'm new at this stealing thing."

Sitting at the wheel, on top of my paper bag full of money, I put the car in gear and head south. I kind of like this hearse; after all, if you are going to kill someone, it's good to have the right car to hide the corpse. The kid grins. He saved me again.

While I'm speeding in the hearse, I think of the hospital. The doctors didn't understand me. My problem is not the cancer, the cancer is a consequence. The problem has a Russian name and oceanic blue eyes. As the evening fades into night, I have to hurry before my problem is already dead.

Fish Silver

The list I wrote was in front of me in a room at the local offices of the House Un-American Activities Committee. Two FBI agents sat in front of me, one scraping a piece of gum from his shoe, the other taking notes. Behind them, there was a big, two-way mirror. I knew the system. Two silhouettes could be seen behind it, but not their faces.

One of the FBI agents calmly dipped a spoon in his coffee, "You shouldn't have written that list."

"Why? What are you going to do to me?"

The two agents looked at each other, confused by my defiance and irreverence. "We can tell you what might happen to you if you don't collaborate by giving names."

"Oh, yeah? What? I could go to jail? You'll threaten my family? How about losing my job? Oh, yeah, I forgot. You can also threaten me about losing my friends because they said my name first. That's an infallible method. People always squeal. The mind is surest weapon."

The agents stared at me, more confused. All of a sudden, from behind the mirrored glass, I thought I heard whistling . "You are my sunshine, my only . . ."

"Daddy? Is that you?" The whistling stopped.

The agents looked at the glass. "What the fuck is going on here?"

An agent came out of a door next to the mirror and ordered, "Let her go."

They gently pushed me out of the room and closed the

door in my face before I could say another word.

———

In the violent, violet sunset, Dmitri and I fished together on the beach. The waves arrived with the motion of heads nodding down the shore, wetting our feet. He was fishing and chewing tobacco. I was fishing and taking notes. It was windless and clean and steady, as if time had stopped its thoughts.

If each one of Dmitri's watches was a story of a person, he wasn't a watch thief after all: he was a story collector like I was. We were the same. I stuck my fishing pole into the sand as though it were a victory flag. Then I realized he had two fish in his bucket, and I had none.

"How will I be able to write about this if I can't catch any fish?"

"Catching a fish is not important. It's enjoying the rhythm of fishing. Like I enjoy sailing even when I don't go anywhere."

"But you don't like to stay in one place, right? "

"I don't know what I like."

"I know what you like. I know things about you even you don't know."

Then he stuck his fishing rod in a hole in the sand. "You think you know."

"What time exactly are you leaving for Mexico tomorrow?"

"I don't know. But I'm surely looking forward to it. Someone said 'Mexico is so far from God and so close to the United States.' "

"I wouldn't know. I hate God anyway."

He was clearly offended, "Then . . . why did you follow me to the church?"

I didn't answer and lowered my fishing rod. He reeled in his line, took his pole out of the sand, and packed all his equipment. "I'm leaving for Mexico right now."

"Now?"

"Are you coming or not? Afraid of the water?"

"I can't leave my job. I like my job, you know."

He left the beach; I followed him to his boat, thinking I didn't have my pajamas, any perfume in case of seasickness, or my favorite pen.

"Why don't you tell me where you're going, and maybe I can catch a later bus?"

"I don't know where I'm going. I'll decide when I get there."

Full of hesitation, I jumped into the boat with him. The wharf moved away without saying good-bye, and I let it go. The sail filled with the night wind, getting round. Scared, I grabbed the mast and slipped down to the deck holding it until I was sitting down. The farther we sailed, the more the boat rocked. The harbor lights shook like drunken fireflies.

Looking for some sort of security, I tied my wrist to the mast with a rope. The boat moved up and down; every time it went down, waves washed over the bow.

"This is what I do, see? Don't write. Just observe." Dmitri said.

There were no colors in the middle of the ocean, or at least I couldn't see any.

"I like to be in the middle of nothing. The sensation of blue all around me. Water and sky are the same blue somedays," he said. "Only the sails and the clouds to stare at. I don't try to find images in the clouds, like overly analytical people do. I just watch them—how big they are, how they move, how far they must be from me, how they change. I can spend the whole afternoon following a maze of clouds, even if it's windy. I can spend hours like that, watching the clouds spreading out, building up, fading, growing dark, changing. I can spend hours talking to myself, hearing the sound of the silence, the sound of water."

"Do you have any more watch stories?"

"Were you listening to what I said?"

"Yes, but do you have more stories or not?"

"So you insist on writing? I stole this watch from a police officer in Louisiana," he showed me the watch he was wearing.

As I started to write, he jiggled the helm. My pen traveled across the page, and he smirked.

"The band is made of alligator skin. The cop made it himself. The guy put a trap with a chicken inside it on the edge of the bayou and waited. When the alligator jumped, he shot it in the stomach. That night, he cut it open and ate the insides."

As I tried to write, he turned to starboard, right, and then to port, left, zigzagging. I wrote what he had said and added to it:

> It's a nice watch. The band is not well glued, though, because he didn't use the right adhesive. I hate when watches

aren't done right, as much as I hate . . . as I hate . . .

I looked up from my notebook and saw he had stopped chewing tobacco and was looking at me with a bored expression. "Why do you have to write all the time?" He spit the tobacco into a mason jar.

"Ever heard of *You are what you do?*" I had read it in some cheap book of phrases.

"Then let's do something." He passed me a fishing rod. "Fishing is nice here, like we're in a cradle." He moved his eyes strangely from his fishing pole to his feet.

"What?" I asked him.

"Nothing."

He turned his eyes, fixing them on the sea. Slate gray waves swept by with cream white foam tops. Whispering, he was pretending everything was all right, but I knew it wasn't because he had forgotten to put bait on his hook.

Finally he grumbled, "What you are is not what you do, it's how you think, the stories you carry inside, with your own way of seeing them, not the ones you borrow from others. What makes you special are the little things: like your thick eyebrows when they arch because you're mad, or your funny way of hating everything."

I didn't think I had thick eyebrows, or that I needed to be exposed to such a lesson. "That sounds like a bunch of crap that people say who don't like their jobs. What do you know about *doing* anyway? You aren't a Communist leader. Hell, you're not even a fisherman because you don't catch shit."

"Are you suggesting I change jobs, Ma'am?" He kicked

the boat.

"No. You shouldn't. With my script, people are going to see you differently. Better, I mean."

"What people?"

"Everybody."

"But the wharf guys like me just fine. When someone tells me something, I listen. If someone is hungry, I share my food. If a person looks at me, I look back. If I feel like moving from a place, I just leave. I don't think in reasons, I only do. I know more about doing than you do. Maybe I'm not better than you, but . . ."

"You *should* think you're better than everyone. Attitude is contagious."

"Who the hell do you think you are to tell me how I am supposed to think?"

"I know how you think."

"I'm not who you think I am."

"But of course you are."

He didn't answer but kept his angry face, and I didn't understand why. He came about suddenly, returning to shore at a fierce pace. The ocean stared at us like a cold giant. His madness intrigued me so much, I forgot I felt dizzy.

When we arrived at the wharf, he threw my things out, including my notebook. I jumped out of the boat and knelt down to gather them. He stopped at the hatchway and turned around to face me. "I'm not gonna rob no more. Or sail. Have to learn a lot of things. Can't stand your writing all day and your do-something talk. You . . . uh . . . I just can't . . . There's something I want to learn and to do it. I'm gonna become a priest. I don't want you to write about me any-more."

A fake fisherman and bad thief who wants conversion? Now that was too much. What was it that he had to learn?

As he entered the cabin, I forced myself to wait on the wharf. I didn't sneak onto the boat, didn't call his name, didn't spy through the windows.

As my hair blew in the wind, I observed the corpse of the vast sea all around me; the stilted, endless beach; the stiff sky. In the quietness, the stubborn, dark ocean swung back and forth, back and forth, insistent.

Increasingly I convinced myself I was going to finish my script no matter who or what was against it. I wasn't Catholic, but I knew who this guy God was. How the hell was I going to compete with God?

Black and White

The church where Dmitri had prayed was demolished; only a dry plain eats at the horizon. A couple of cows graze nearby. I like their combination of colors. Black and white, opposites, the colors don't mingle at all. Some things will never mingle. White is white and black is black. I focus on the darkest, blackest spot on one cow.

"The church was here? Are you sure?" the kid asks, and I nod.

Behind the old church ruins, there is a convent. "Why not ask there?" the kid says, so I follow.

In the convent's stone courtyard, there is a herd of nuns wearing their habits. A labyrinth of women dressed completely in black. They walk in circles, synchronized, heads down, praying, muttering, making little, childlike sounds. Could it be a rite against me?

I think of the nuns as cows, same colors, same round shape.

I like nuns because they hide from their own emotions. They extinguish their feelings.

"Do you think you would recognize him?" the kid asks me.

"Of course," I say, although I'm not so sure. I try to remember if his eyes were blue or gray, if his face was round or oval, if his cheek bones were prominent or not. At least I'm sure he was blond. Maybe I control my feelings, but obviously not my mind. Some events remain in my mind as clear as day, and others escape like floating balloons. Memories come back when they want, not when I need them. Memory is a son-of-a-bitch.

I grab one of the nuns by her habit, pulling her out of the procession. "Excuse me, I'm in kind of a hurry . . . I'm in a bit of a spot here. God or somebody must have sent you. I'm looking for a man . . ."

"I don't know any men," the nun says, pulling back the sleeve of her habit and walking away to join the others.

Completely out of control now, I dart into the middle of the circle and yell, "Can someone help me?" Their black-and-white habits spin around me like ghosts. Then I try to stop a few other nuns, but they don't even hear me because they are engrossed in prayer, so I sit discouraged on the raised roots of a large tree; the kid sits beside me.

From a doorway I see a young nun come out who walks with her feet open like a clock at ten to two. She has a clean, white transparent face and docile, caramel-colored eyes.

"May I help you?"

"I'm looking for a person, Sister. A man. He's tall, muscular, tanned, blond hair, blue eyes. I think."

"I don't know anyone who fits that description. I'm sorry."

"Well, maybe he doesn't have blond hair any more, what about white hair, wrinkled pale face, very old, and probably skinny?"

"What's his name, Ma' am?"

"Dmitri. Or maybe you know him as Joe." I mumble, staring at her peaceful crucifix.

"Joe, the old fisherman?"

"Old?" I gape down at the kid. He laughs.

"Yes, Ma' am, we call him that. He tells the best stories I've ever heard. Stories about the sea and watches."

"That's the one. I also heard his stories about the world. Did he finally become a priest here?"

The nun laughs out loud. "The old sailor liked life too much to be in a jail like this," she giggles, "God was inside of him wherever he went. Although he didn't travel around the world. Only to Mexico once. I think someone else told him the stories."

"Who?"

"I don't know."

What a schmuck, to lie to me about the origin of the stories, too. He really deserved to die, like my father. Only this time I'm not going to ask God for it, I'll handle it myself.

The nun grabs a bucket and waters the apple green flowers along the path. "He took some classes to become a priest, but he was always telling his stories more than studying. Good man, though. Spent the last twenty years helping the order."

Twenty years? That's not how I pictured his past. If I had been here, I would have told him not to do that.

"Where is he?"

"I don't know."

Thanks a lot, ugly rag head, I want to say, but instead, I smile, "Is he alive?"

"I don't know. His son is a priest here, if you want to ask him," she says, pointing at the confessional.

Just as I look at the mysterious wooden box, the doors open, and a beaming, white face shines out as if its light came from within. He doesn't look like Dmitri; he has a flat face, dark skin, dark hair, dark eyes. He reminds me of someone else, but I'm not sure who. As he gets out of the confessional, I notice he is about six feet tall, two feet taller than I. What am I going to tell him from down here?

"Hi. Uh . . . I knew your father. The truth of the matter is that now I'm not so sure I knew him. At least, I didn't know the same person who was your father."

Someone pulls at my dress; I look down and see the kid pointing at the young priest, "He could be my father, couldn't he?"

Dmitri's son kneels in front of the kid. "You don't have one? We have kids like you here. We can all be your dad. I mean, we could, only if you want to."

"Look, kid, stop searching for your fucking dad and grow up. We all end up alone anyway."

The kid runs away, a mixture of scared and sad, so I turn around and stare into Dmitri's son's eyes. I'm still waiting for the answer: where the hell is he?

"I'm sorry, I haven't seen my dad for a while. Maybe two years."

"Two years?" Everything feels like a nightmare. The nuns, who are parading in a circle around me, start to make me feel dizzy. One old nun lifts up a Bible and calls to the sky. Damn. I don't know how they can be so passionate about God. I can't believe they follow someone they don't know and who never answers. I can't believe I follow a man who never answered either.

Impatient, I scowl at Dmitri's son. "Do you have any idea where can I find your father?"

"Last I saw him, he was at the Saint Vincent retirement home. It's fifteen miles east of here, in West Covina, but as I said, that was two months ago. I don't know if he's still there."

"He has to be. Thanks. Bye."

"What about the kid? Can he stay with us?"

The kid's in the middle of the nuns' procession, as if he were one himself. As I grab the kid's arm, he yells, "I'm not leaving. I want to have lunch with them! I saw lots of bread and chicken soup and potatoes and meatballs in their kitchen."

"Learn to get a hold of yourself. Wishes can wait."

"Maybe yours can!"

A group of kids runs to a long table, playing and screaming. They seem well fed and happy.

"Do you really want to stay, kid?"

"Do you want me to stay?"

"Well, I'm going to need a copilot. And you're pretty good in that department."

"I don't want to leave you."

"Maybe I don't want you to leave me, either."

We walk to the exit, and on the way out, the kid steals a handful of hosts from a goblet on a small altar in the courtyard.

Pushing him, I sit him inside the car and carefully put on his seat belt. We drive east.

"Are you going to die?" he asks, eating a host.

"Perhaps."

"Are you going to go to hell?"

"Hell, I hope not. Anyway, I don't give a damn if I am."

"I'm going to go to hell," the kid mutters. "It's not my personal opinion, Mom told me so."

"Your mom's full of shit." The kid stares at me, surprised, and then grins. I grin, too. "How old is she?"

"I don't know. Maybe eighty."

"Eighty? Then how old do you think I am?"

The kid looks around with his eyes wide open. He has no clue. He bites his lip, wondering. "Seven hundred?"

I laugh, but then I feel a piercing stab in my chest that forces me to bend forward. I put my right hand on my heart, but I don't let go of the wheel with my shaky left.

"How far are we from the retirement home, kid? I don't think I'm going to make it."

I had promised Dmitri I wouldn't write about him any more if we had dinner one more time as a good-bye. For some reason, he hadn't mentioned becoming a priest again, but I knew it was still on his mind—every night he made the sign of the cross on his chest, and sometimes, he tightened a napkin on his neck. I knew I had to fight that idea. The only way to defy God is with lust.

It was a perfect, warm afternoon for seduction. While the impatient fireflies waited to glow, I shaved my legs in the sink. My hair had gotten much longer. Watching myself in the mirror, I brushed my hair like Veronica Lake, put some of my mother's fruit-scented cologne on my chest, and slipped into my tight, cotton, coral, flowered dress for the first night of my life.

Stubborn as a mule, I showed up at his boat with a sex scene from my screenplay to read to him and a bottle of his favorite beer. He lay on a shabby cushion, I was beside him on a rattan chair, and we drank on the deck, scanning the stars with a certain sense of eternity. When, after several beers the eager night arrived, everything we talked about seemed to make sense.

"I like the Pacific," Dmitri muttered, pointing to the horizon. Our sky seemed clearer than on any other that night, and I wondered what color it was, but couldn't decipher it.

"I can look at the Pacific for hours," he muttered, "if I

look too long at the Atlantic, I feel lost." Then he told me that his eyes were originally gray, and that their color had been transformed over the years to blue—from looking so long at the ocean. He said that the blue of the Pacific was contagious like a disease.

"What are you most afraid of?" I asked him, thinking about the word *disease*. Waiting for his answer, I stared right into his eyes and let the right sleeve of my dress slide down, exposing my naked shoulder.

He scratched his head, puzzled. "I don't know if I'm afraid of this, but I don't like it when people leave me. I guess that's why I travel, to leave them first. And you?"

"I'm afraid that no one will differentiate me from others. And I'm afraid of death, but no more than anybody else."

He gazed at his toes. I stared at him. His eyes were so intense, so bizarre, so far from me. It wasn't just their painfully itching, blue color. His eyes seemed to hide things. I put my foot next to his.

"You know, if you become a priest you'll deprive yourself of some great things . . ." I said seductively.

"I know what you mean, like sailing places."

"I wasn't talking about that . . ."

I took out my notebook and read him a section from my screenplay. It was a scene about desire, so I stood up and read it out loud, my chin up, my cleavage bare as I moved my hands passionately. Deeply insecure, I tried to make my voice masculine, rough, sexy:

My stormy veins and shivering pores want to disembark
on your mouth. Your cushioned stubborn lips. My desires

visit me, but the nets over these neglected limbs won't let them in. . . .

Once finished, I took a long pause, hiding my face with the notebook, and then fixing my eyes on his. I was afraid that he wouldn't like it, afraid he wouldn't like how I described him. I sensuously fluttered my eyelashes.

"Ohhhh, now I know what you meant by not being able to do things . . . Those people in your book, they really know how to . . . I never did that like that."

"You've never done it?"

"No. I've never done it with women."

I was clearly disappointed. "There's nothing wrong with liking men."

"But I don't."

"Who did you do it with then?"

"Sheep, things like that, in the country, some time ago."

So I had to save him from celibacy, God, and animals? I sat down in the chair, slouching. We remained silent, I looking at my notebook without seeing.

"Great guy," he remarked about the character. "We have a lot in common, you know, we both work on a boat."

When he didn't realize that the guy was himself, I gaped at him furiously. "I guess so." I had thought words could influence people to make them want things, but the problem was I didn't know enough about sex to write about it.

He rolled over on his cushion and flipped through a magazine. I wasn't going to give up on lust, so I got up out of the chair and pointed to his cushion, "I'm allergic to your rattan chair. May I sit with you?" I lied so I could sit closer to him, because I believed that if I sat closer he would begin to desire me.

He stood, offering me the shabby cushion, "It's okay, Ican sit in the chair."

For a moment, I caught his eye, trying to divine what he was thinking, and then gave up, lowering my head. Then I swung my hair backwards, hoping he'd smell my lemon shampoo. I let my small ears show. I stretched my right arm close to his face, trying to look casual. I extended my fingers. Nothing worked.

"My arm is stiff. You seem tense, too," I whispered and slid my fingers across his back.

"I'm not tense," he took my hand off.

Then I crossed my legs, and then crossed my arms on my hips. I wasn't going to let him harm me; I could take care of hurting myself whenever I wanted to, but he wouldn't and couldn't.

If he left me, I'd be like a fishhook without bait. His bait was the watches and the stories of the people who wore them. But if he didn't like me, why had he stolen my watch? What was the story of my watch? Why had he chosen me?

"You never ask me about myself. Aren't you interested?'

He looked down. I wanted to surrender but couldn't.

"How come you never told me anything about the other scenes I gave you to read?"

"Maybe tomorrow."

He always said "tomorrow." After a while, he started to play with a small turquoise blue plastic ball, smiling like a child, making it bounce on the wall. A part of me believed I just wanted my character to stay so I could keep writing about him, but I also wanted the *real him* to stay with me.

Opposing ocean currents moved the boat. I felt that maybe I could stay with him forever, but I kept telling myself I didn't love him. Not yet.

Swallowing my thoughts, I closed the boat's portholes, shutting the curtains tight. "Tomorrow is fine," I whispered awkwardly. Or maybe I didn't say anything, because he didn't answer, and kept playing with his ball. He stared at the deck, and I wondered what he was thinking, if he was upset with me. I thought about the sea, how solitary it is, how boundless, beautiful, and blue. Then, I focused on his bare feet as they tapped the floor—they had thick veins and seemed strong. I wondered if they were cold.

And I wondered why what I felt for him felt so much like fear.

Without warning, the ball bounced off my head. Dmitri approached and kissed me on the forehead, telling me beautiful things. I wish I could remember what. He held my hands, lowered his eyes, and I could see him closely, so close I shivered. Suddenly I embraced him tightly, trying to squeeze out of myself what I felt for him.

In my opinion, playing with that ball was stupid, but I started playing with him. I threw it back and forth; we played for a while, and he even let me win once. I laughed a lot that night, forgetting about time, forgetting myself.

As we said good-bye on the wharf, he stared at me and grinned broadly. I smiled back, realizing I was smiling the way he did, showing my gums and all my teeth.

"I'm sorry I can't stay up late, I have to pack for tomorrow," he said, reaffirming himself.

"So you're leaving for sure? Good luck, then."

As soon as we both turned around, my smile languished, and my eyes filled with a strangely sweet fog.

Blood Brown

I learned the difference between lies and truth the day my father died.

Pa, Ma, and I were strolling down one of those tiny cobblestone alleys with dirty, old buildings and lots of small balconies. Pa swaggered in between us while Ma and I each held one of his hands. No one talked. There was an obvious tension between Pa and me, so Mama tried to cheer us up....

"I can't wait to see the famous kiss between Burt Lancaster and Deborah Kerr."

With a fatherly gesture, Pa caressed my hair, and I don't know why I let him. Then Pa and Ma stepped off the curb; they waited for me to follow. Looking at the ground, I placed my small, patent leather shoe on the concrete and heard a gunshot. Pa's hand slid out of mine. As I turned to him, I saw his body folding. His forehead made a dry thud on the cobblestones.

Gasping, I looked up to where the shot had come from. A silhouette of a young man with a gun left his hiding place. A ray of light blinded me for a second, and then I saw that the man was wearing a red bandanna. When I took a step farther, he mirrored me, stepping farther forward. I clearly recognized Dmitri's face. Our eyes locked for a moment. Then he violently turned and ran away, disappearing before I could open my mouth.

I was frozen, eyes wide open, until Pa's painful shriek pulled me out of shock, and I knelt down by his side, wrapping him in my arms. A tear fell down my cheek, I wiped it right away.

Pa lay there in agonizing pain in the middle of the street, grasping at the sidewalk with his fingers. Ma howled and cried and screamed. No head appeared from any of the balconies. No door was opened. No one wanted to be an accomplice in saving a man who deserved to die.

"They won't open. They know he's a rat, Mom. Everybody knows but you."

Without listening, Ma grabbed me by the shoulders, "I'm going to call an ambulance. You stay here, take care of your father. Talk to him while I go find someone to help us."

"What should I tell him?"

"Anything . . . I don't know . . . make up something . . . lie if you want," she yelled, running away. "If you talk to him and keep him busy thinking, he won't die."

Hugging his shaking body, I stared at him. His round eyes, rigid. Lids trembling from the sides. Body stiff as a bare tree limb. Trembling mouth dripping blood. For the first time, he seemed so vulnerable. I wondered if he would still be mean when he was dead. Ma had said Pa wasn't bad; she said the alcohol made him bad. I should talk to him so he doesn't die, I thought.

Hesitant, I bent over him, bringing my mouth to his ear. I stayed still just breathing, without knowing what to say. Then I looked at his dried, yellowing lips—the ones that told me so many lies—and I remembered the words that had come out of them: The only way to survive is to kill first. I stared at his ring finger rubbing the concrete—the one that had slapped me so many times. I said nothing.

Stiff as a statue, I stood up, swallowing my thoughts. No more alcohol for you, Daddy. No more vodka and orange juice. No more orange. No more.

Observing him, I remained frozen beside his body. His blood ran out quickly, tinting his blond hair, flowing onto the cobblestones like muddy rain. I stood there for what seemed hours, watching the blood spread. The sound of water washing something down the street.

Mama ran from one place to another, yelling for help, and all I did was stare at his blood. I learned the difference between lies and truth seeing that blood. Blood is not carmine, it is not tomato, not dark orange. Blood is not red. Blood is brown. If you wait until it is dried you can see that. The only way to see the truth about anything is by waiting.

———

The same day Pa died, Mom was committed to a mental hospital. She just couldn't bear to be without him. I was stronger; I could bear anything. I know that I cried when my father died, yet not because I was sad, but because of all the fear I had had before.

She was crazy and I was alone. She was in a private mental hospital in Beverly Hills, which I would visit from 8 to 9 A.M. When I arrived, she was already drunk. Her almost bold, dyed-auburn-red-hair was disheveled, her eyes shrimp pink and swollen, and her smile stuck on. Incredible, eight in the morning and already drunk! I couldn't find the bottles, so I guessed she paid some nurse. She always paid people to get whatever she wanted.

When I went to visit her, I brought makeup and a brush she loved. I knew I had one hour. So the first twenty minutes I used to make her up and brush her hair, just in case someone was coming. We both knew nobody would come. Then I spoke for ten minutes about our house. And the last half hour, I let her talk. She said the things she generally said—reproaches at the beginning, fading into melancholic memories about Pa and Italy. Then she would remind me how much he loved me, how many things he had given me, all the books, remind me of the day they had an argument because of how much he loved me, of how he wouldn't call me Carla, but instead, Carlina, of how much Pa used to like my sleeping between them.

I wanted to tell her that she had told me the same things a million times. But I didn't say anything, and I thought, Pa was a son-of-a-bitch, Mama, don't you remember? He died because he deserved it, because I wanted him to die, that's why. Italy wasn't better than this, Mama, don't you remember? You don't remember anything. What you are telling me is not your life, it's someone else's, or no one's. I don't remember. I don't remember if I was my father's favorite. I don't remember if I was happy. One can skillfully learn to forget.

We didn't talk about what I wrote. She didn't understand books or screenplays or letters, or why people write.

When my mother committed suicide that day at noon, I was surprised—I always had thought I would die before my parents. She left me a bag with three thousand dollars in twenty-dollar bills, but I never touched it; the money is in the paper bag just as she left it.

Luckily, I couldn't stay long at her wake with the rest of

the family. I was bored because I couldn't count colors in the crowd. Black won.

Lilac

"Now you've done it, kid!" We stop beside the road in the middle of an almost deserted town, so far east of Los Angeles it smells of straw, and the silence belongs to the flies and the wind. "How can you vomit in the car! You need a doctor. I'm the one who should be throwing up, not you."

A tangle of colors slides on the seat. "I'm sorry I got sick. You drive too slowly and move from one side of the road to the other," the kid whines, opening the glove compartment where the gun is. I close it instantaneously.

He takes off his sweater and starts wiping the seat with it. "I wanted to tell you to go faster, but I was afraid you'd kick me out on the road."

"Well, I have to leave you now. It's better this way. Find someone who can love you. Find someone who can love."

I don't glance at him, but away from him, and see a couple of annoying American kids sitting on the sidewalk; their little fists tap on the curb to the rhythm of a song. Didn't your mother tell you not to sit on the sidewalk? That's why I'm not a mother; I would make a lousy one. Their green socks don't match their turquoise shorts. I let the damned kids keep singing their song. In Los Angeles, kids usually don't sit on the sidewalk; maybe they do in Mexico, but here kids have to act like adults. While the kid keeps wiping the seat, the sun glares off the road and slaps my face, so I take my old, yellowing notebook from the bag and shade my forehead, protecting myself from all light and people.

"All right, kid. You're a tiny bit better than other kids."
I throw his sweater in the back and start cleaning with a yellowing letter I wrote to Dmitri.

"I'm sorry, I didn't mean to barf," the kid trembles with his eyes down. "One of the candy bars I ate must've been bad."

"How many did you eat?"

"Twenty. Maybe nineteen."

"Have you eaten twenty candy bars?" Noticing all the empty, lilac candy wrappers on the car floor, I count them. Ten on the floor of the back seat; eight, nine, ten near the kid's slippers. He kicks them. "Twenty? You're lucky, kid! If I were you, I'd be dead. Now I'll take a painkiller, and you can take a couple of Alka Seltzers."

I offer him the last sip of what's left of my soda.

"I can't believe how skinny you are with all that you ate. Well, don't worry, your body will stretch to the sides when you reach around thirty, and it won't stop, unless you get cancer."

"Is it easy to get cancer?"

"Easier than you think. You can basically get it living your life with a good daily dose of anger."

A police car passes next to us, slows down, and turns on its siren. Pulling over, I freeze on the seat. Will he notice our car is stolen? My shoulders shrink as I look in the rearview mirror and see an officer wearing fake, mirrored Ray Bans, looking at the hearse's license plate. He takes notes and talks on his police radio.

I fix the Mexican hat on my head, glance at the clock in

the car, and then look toward the end of the road.

As I see the policeman approaching us in the rearview mirror, I grab a melted lipstick from my purse, rub my index finger on it, and cover my teeth with it. The cop leers at me through the window. I roll it down and show him my yellowing teeth covered with red spots.

"Any problem officer?

"We're looking for a car just like this. Can I see your license and registration, Ma'am?"

"Miss."

My eyes move nervously out of control from side to side; I don't have either; I don't remember if I ever did.

"I must've forgotten them at home. It happens."

"You're gonna have to come with me to the station then."

The policeman's walkie-talkie goes off . . .

"The plates don't match."

"See?" I lift an eyebrow.

"You still have to come with me because you forgot your license."

"Just write me a ticket and let me off. If you don't have a good reason to arrest me, I'm sure my lawyer will be happy to collect money from the police department."

I pretend to cough, and the policeman looks at me compassionately, waving us off. Still shaky, I watch the patrol car disappear down the road.

"People don't think an old lady could steal, much less kill."

The kid leans against the window. "They couldn't tell the

car was stolen because I changed the plates with another hearse's from the funeral home." Smiling mischievously, he shows me the other license plate.

"That's what they want you to think, kid, but the cops are planning something worse for me. Just like the Feds back then. All national authorities are the same. That's why I don't want you to need me. Don't worry about cleaning up. Get out. They're gonna find me sooner or later. You're free to go."

He steps down and just stands on the road. The clanging hearse moves slowly onto the road again. In the rearview mirror I see the kid crying, getting smaller and smaller as I get farther away from him.

Frowning, I make U-turn and go back to him. The kid silently jumps in the car, drying his tears.

I glance seriously at the clock, move my hurting back, and cough. The kid imitates my actions. He gazes seriously at the clock, exaggerates a cough, and then squints to the end of the road.

"What do you think you are doing?" I ask angrily.

"I'm learning how to become an old person with cancer."

"That's not old, that's stupid."

"Have you done stupid things?"

I don't answer but turn off the engine.

"Why don't you want me?"

"It's not that, kid. I don't want you to want *me*."

I turn on the radio with the volume very loud. The kid rolls down his window and sticks his head out, letting the wind stream across his face. He starts to whimper silently. Tears drip down his round, pink cheeks, leaving two dirt traces. He doesn't wipe them and doesn't wail or moan, just lets them fall.

What can I tell him? When you love someone you become stupid. Na! I can't tell him that. Two, and then three, tractor-trailers pass us, and their blasts shake the hearse.

I don't even glance at the kid, but I know he keeps crying. Even if I wanted to, I couldn't cry; my tears are imprisoned somewhere inside with a lock I wouldn't know how to open.

"You know, kid? I haven't cried in forty-something years. My throat must be covered with salty, dry tears."

The kid draws letters with his finger on the dirty window. He writes F-A-T-H-E-R and the wipes it off angrily.

"All right, kid, you win. Ask again."

He wipes the tears from his nose with the sleeve of his T-shirt, "I asked if you've done stupid things."

"Everybody's done some."

"Did you?"

"You bet."

"Like what?"

"Well, when you love someone, you do a lot of things that aren't exactly . . . that are . . . how can I say it . . . dumb."

"You mean that when you're in love anything goes?"

"Unfortunately, by the time you realize this, you'll be too old to do anything about it."

"How will I know when I'm old?"

"When you talk too much, don't listen, ramble, and answer questions no one has asked."

"How many stupid things do I have to do to be really old?"

"Maybe a lot. Maybe just one. I got old when I was nineteen."

"What did you do? What? Dmitri didn't leave that day like you told me?"

"No. He didn't leave that day. And we didn't say goodbye without kisses."

"I knew you lied to me."

"I didn't lie, just changed things around a little so they would be more entertaining. I just told you the censored version. I was afraid to tell you the truth."

Pure White

A white Sunday. Ten or eleven at night. Forty-nine years ago.

Nervously pacing back and forth in my room, I decide to put on a white blouse and a white cotton skirt. White renewed me. If he and his God didn't like my lust, I had to get rid of those feelings; after all, I had all my life ahead to forget him.

But first I had to clarify my father's death with him. When I arrived at the wharf, I saw him in the distance before he saw me. He was lying down on his boat, covered by a mat. The windows were closed. The warm, inviting light was on inside.

In the fog, spotlights from two ships made shadows, suddenly making me realize I was being followed by two FBI agents.

Afraid, I started to run down the wharf to his boat. They chased me, having longer legs than mine.

At soon as Dmitri saw me in the distance, I motioned for him to hide. Luckily, he got inside his boat, unseen. Eventually, the agents caught up with me.

"Why were you running, Miss?"

"You scared me."

"What's a girl like you doing in this neighborhood? Were you meeting a Commie by any chance?"

"No one, so you can leave now. "

The agents cornered me against Dmitri's boat. I wondered if, from inside, he could hear what they said.

"Look, lady, we're just doing our jobs. Some Americans are doing what they shouldn't be doing."

"Naming names, that's what they should be doing?"

"I'm not going to answer that because you're a woman."

"I understand. You won't answer me because to your understanding, I am inferior."

"Let's go, Jack, this gal is nuts."

They walked away. When they were far enough away, Dmitri peeked out and invited me to come in.

Once inside, he poured me a shot of whiskey, and I drank it more quickly than usual.

"I thought you weren't interested in politics, Carla. Thank you for covering up for me."

I sat close to him, holding a cold bottle of beer between my legs. Above the water, an ochre fog strolled in. Within the mysterious fog, we saw the shadows of other boats passing by.

"Why'd you kill my father?"

"I did it for you. Otherwise he was gonna beat the shit out of you and kick you out of the country. You wanted him dead."

"What? How did you know?"

"Sometimes you think out loud. In church, you asked God to kill him. And I knew God wasn't gonna do it for you."

I nodded. "I didn't mean for you to do it. Thanks, I guess."

He looked at me, surprised. "Why not me?" he said, his voice slowed from to much beer. "No one ever defended me.

No one followed me like that. In fact, no one gave a damn about me, not even my mother. She dumped me. Although sometimes you're cold with me like the morning ocean."

I wrote that down. It was better than any of my phrases.

He grabbed my notebook, taking it from me. "You and your little book . . ."

"I'm almost finished, you know? It's a pity you're leaving. I'll have to fill in the rest with lies."

He took the notebook and started reading. From time to time, he lifted his eyebrow and nodded, smiling.

Then he went to the last page and started reading that. I followed his eyes as they moved from one side to the other, as he frowned and nodded once in a while. He looked so vulnerable reading; the way he stared so seriously at the page made me want to hug him.

> You dash away from me guided by a shimmering Latin breeze. I want to tickle your slippery toe tips, knowing nothing but our stare. I'm from nowhere and belong to no one, but you smell like home.

"This is great," he put down the notebook. "It's really, really funny."

Funny? I was convinced it was hollow. "Do you really think it's great?"

"Yeah."

He had never paid so much attention to me; so I attributed the fascination to the beer.

"I'm glad you won't abandon me, I mean, that you won't leave the idea of writing about me. And I like how your mouth pouts, stubborn like."

I was so frozen that I moved my neck around and it cracked. "My back hurts."

"May I fix it? I'm good at that."

Dmitri approached me, slipped his hands under my blouse, and dug his thumbs into my back. He massaged my skinny shoulders. His fingertips were as soft as cotton. Why the hell I told him my back hurt, I don't know. I felt warm. I let him do it.

"How old are you?" he asked me for the first time.

"Who cares!"

"I do."

I wondered if he really cared about me. "No more than sixteen," I said lying, finding it kind of romantic that he would go to jail because of me, but romanticism exists only in art. There's no romanticism in real life, so I told the truth, "I'm nineteen, three months, and twenty-one days."

"Lie down," he said, instead of telling me how old he was. I stared at his blackish-blue eyes. They seemed kind of ashy gray that night, like wasted rubber. He had the hardest eyes, the hardest, the coldest, the most mysterious.

Would I ever know what was really in his mind? I wondered.

Every little sound was denser than ever: the grunting of confused fish; the bewildered breaking of the waves, their intriguing bubbles bursting.

I lay on the floor face down, and he gave me an ugly, orange towel to put under myself. I took it just the same. After all, he never knew my feelings about orange.

He continued his caresses on the skin of my back, the bones of my legs, my feet, and my toes. One by one. I started to have shameless thoughts and rested my chin on my hands as I scanned the room: one red bottle on the table, two ripe tomatoes: three reds. I looked back and saw his inviting juicy red lips: four reds . . . or was it five?

I tried to keep my attention outside. I looked to the window. The fog drifted, muffling the ocean sounds.

It's not so bad if I just kiss him, I thought. I didn't know how to do the rest anyway. I turned my head around, glancing at his hands on my shoulders.

Kiss me, kiss me, I thought. Maybe I had drunk more than I should have, so I mumbled, "My back doesn't hurt any more. I think I'm okay now."

He pulled his hands off me. Stupid, stupid, I thought, pulled my blouse down and sat up. He turned the phonograph on; a love song played and he turned the volume up a little. I always hated corny songs; they always keep repeating the word "heart." I awkwardly looked around; he looked around, too, away from me. Usually, the things our minds need the most our bodies find unattainable.

His silences were as cold as his winter gaze. I couldn't understand him, couldn't communicate. There was no way I could ever tame him to be like me. He was wild and vulgar and ordinary and delightfully simple. I hated his long silences.

"So?" I muddled.

"So what?" he asked.

We both smiled at each other, and then he burst out

laughing. A lousy laugh, loud and noisy like hiccups—lousy but funny. I kept on giggling like a silly girl. It wasn't funny any more, but I didn't know what else to do. Still laughing, he came closer. I felt idiotic, stupid, dumb, and more idiotic. Somehow I let him get closer. His face inched in front of mine; his eyes hurt my insides.

"What are you thinking?" I asked.

Calmly he kissed my hands—each one of my fingertips and then all over my palms. I tried to recreate his thoughts—he should have been thinking something. As he kept on kissing my palms, I kept on trying to figure out what was he thinking. *The sea . . . you . . . the fingers . . . fingers . . .* He slowly ran his fingers along my lips as he said, "I think you're pretty. I think you're interesting and smart. I think I'd like to be with you for a long, long time. I think you're the one."

"I know you're the one." I jumped up and embraced him and caressed his cheeks and his eyelids and passionately pressed my lips on his. He kissed me back. The boat rocked.

He kissed me all over my neck and my nape, caressing my hair, crooking his fingers in it. He said he was going to do "the coral and the jewel." He said he learned it from an Indian who knew the Kamasutra. Said that in Katmandu, the lips are the coral and the teeth are the jewel, the soft biting is called . . . I softly pressed my index finger on his mouth.

His wide eyes stared at me so intensely, I closed mine. As he softly bit my skin, pulling it, I lifted my hand to stop him because it felt too good. Taking my hand away, he rubbed his lips against mine. Letting my thoughts go, I lifted his T-shirt, placing my head under it, like under a tent, and running my nose from his cushiony chest to his muscular belly. He didn't smell like I thought he would, not bad, just different, like baby powder.

Staring at me, he nibbled across my back, touching me in spots I didn't even know I had. He knew what he was doing. I opened my eyes, glancing up, and saw his shadow on the wall as he took off his T-shirt. Then he undid the buttons of my blouse one by one and slid it off my shoulders. No, no, no, I thought, although I meant yes, yes, yes.

When he came back to my lower lip and bit it slowly, I kissed him steadily, leaning back. He embraced my skinny chest with the big eagle tattooed on his. I closed my eyes tight, made a fist, and didn't hear guilty thoughts any more, only the rhythm of his breath. Then, I embraced his waist with my legs making the hardest frontier around him. He rubbed his face all over my chest going down and down. While he kissed my belly, I pressed his shoulders, and his fingertips searched in the silence. It felt so good that I couldn't count how many times I kissed him or how many minutes it took. I couldn't count anything anymore. The water lapped the impermeable hull over and over.

That was the first time I made love, kid. For him, it was the first too. But for me, it was also the last.

―――

When I woke up, I got out of bed silently, without waking him up. Because Dmitri slept on oblivious, and because I knew he was leaving that day, I just wrote a note: "Good-bye, dear thief." Then I looked at the note and tore it up. I left quickly, hoping he would think that what happened had all been a strange dream.

A couple of hours later, I entered my office with the biggest of all grins. As I approached my desk, I saw my things in a box. Markins put his hand on my shoulder in a conde scending manner.

"I told you, dear. Why did you mention so many impor-tant names on your dumb list?"

"Oh, please. Don't take my job away. Not now. I don't have anything else to . . . I promise I won't write anymore lists."

"I'm sorry, darling, but someone has written a list with your name on it."

"I know. That son-of-a-bitch my father. Before he died, he must've . . ."

"What are you talking about? If it hadn't been for your father, you would've lost this job a long time ago. He kept you off of any lists."

I was frozen with confusion. "Father defended me? I thought . . ."

"You didn't know? Well, now that he's gone, no one will protect you. I'm so sorry, darling. It's not my decision, but you can't work in Hollywood any more."

"I'll look for another job in New York."

"You don't understand. Your name is with all the studios, agencies, theaters. No one in this country will give you a job. It's an order from above."

I grabbed my box of things, angrily embraced it, approached the window, and calmly threw out its contents. The little papers fell and fell like summer snow.

As I exited, I looked up at the building, sad and angry at the same time. Then I started walking quickly. Little by little, a smile started forming on my face. Then I started running faster and faster, heading toward the harbor.

As Dmitri untied the ropes and raised the sails, I dashed toward him, running down the wharf as fast as I could. When I got there, I said casually, "So are we leaving then?"

"I thought you were afraid to . . . ? What about your job? Where are your bags?"

"I don't need anything now. . . ."

Soil Black

Once we reach West Covina, we pass tractors and trucks with melons, watermelons, tomatoes, chickens. While the attendant finishes putting gas in our hearse, I look at a map of Los Angeles, trying to figure out the directions the nun gave me to the retirement home. In ten or fifteen minutes, I'll finally wrench away my past.

As I wait, I spot an advertisement for Lancôme on the roadside, where brunette and blonde models hug each other with perfectly tight skin. I stare at the models, then at the bad reflection of myself in the mirror, and I sink deep down in the painful seat.

Whenever you cross a border, beauty is defined differently. Honor is defined differently. Mexicans prefer brunettes, Americans blondes. I wonder what Dmitri preferred, I never asked him. I wonder what he prefers now.

As soon as I can, I hand the man some money so he will leave us alone. I notice that the roots of the trees here are rising like the veins in my hands, curving the black soil.

On the radio, a Mozart opera is playing. The kid switches to a rock 'n' roll station, and I switch it back to the opera. Finally I let him win and listen to whatever he wants. But I won't lose this game with my past.

A patrol car pulls over twenty feet away. Quickly I jostle the wires under the steering wheel, and as it sparks, the engine roars. I roll down the window and spit on the ground a mix of saliva and blood. I'm not stopping anymore.

"Wait," the kid whines, touching his stomach.

"What?"

"I don't feel okay. I think I gotta go shit."

I glare at him; he knows I don't like his vulgar language. He corrects himself, "I have to do some business. You have to help me go to the bathroom."

"What?"

"I don't like to go to the bathroom in gas stations alone."

"You're a young criminal and a car and convenience-store thief, and you're scared of bathrooms?"

"Only in gas stations."

"Look, kid, I can't take care of you. Look at me, I can't even take care of myself. I told you. I don't want you to get used to needing me."

"Please, Miss Carla," the kid pouts.

I grumble and put on some more pearl pink lipstick, looking at myself in the rearview mirror. I focus on my lips. Jesus! Those lips have wrinkles all over them like the deep folds of a long-worn-out skirt.

"Miss Carla . . ."

Impatient, I glance beyond the gas station: an exposed town, about thirty silent houses, fifteen closed stores, eight of which are defunct pharmacies. Behind it, heavy stones, thick bushes, and cactuses stretch into the desert, frightening the elderly town.

I'm not afraid, but my hands shake. I know nothing bad is going to happen when I get to the retirement home. I know he is not going to reject me. I know all that, but I have to go there just to make sure. Because I hate . . . I wondered if I should stop my hatred . . . Shitty town, everything looks embalmed.

"Okay," the kid growls, mad at me, "I'm going alone. And I'll tell you more . . ." he clutches his stomach. "No . . . that's all I have to say." He jumps out of the car, begins to walk toward the bathroom, and stops to threaten me, "I don't know how long I'm gonna take, though."

The two cops get out of their patrol car.

"Oh, no. Don't be long."

"Miss Carla, I think we have to talk."

"Well, I don't."

"My mother used to come with me."

"That's a lie." I stare at him. He stares back, guiltily raising his eyebrows.

"What the hell do *you* know?" the kid grumbles.

"I can smell a lie from a mile. I knew since I was young that the road to death was going to be a long one, full of lies."

Charcoal Green

Dmitri and I moved to Ensenada, but only for two days, during which he didn't talk about being a priest anymore and didn't fish because he wanted me to talk about myself, everything about me. Talking so much about myself and being in that stupid state of mind called love, I couldn't write.

The evening that everything happened, I was cooking a swordfish on an improvised barbecue on the Ensenada beach. Although I dressed simply and maybe even looked happy, I know now I really wasn't. Dmitri, on the other hand, plainly looked sad. He stared at the water, playing with an American flag. His eyes were watery.

"Do you remember the American alleys . . . There are no alleys here," he said. "And there's no one I can really talk to. I mean, I can say a phrase in Spanish here and there, but their humor is different."

"Do you miss it?"

"You don't?"

"I don't have the option of asking myself if I miss it."

With the flag staff, he drew a map of the U.S. in the sand.

"I miss it so much, I think I'd rather be in jail there than free here. I don't know how long I can stay before I go crazy. Let's go back."

"What the fuck are you talking about? You made me come. You killed my father. You made me write that list. You got me fired. I can't go back now."

"I'm sorry. I'm going back eventually. I have to go back.

I miss the wide streets, the quick language. I miss it. I'm not like you. Please come with me."

"Are you willing to lose me for a place?"

"You'll be disappointed in me sooner or later, anyway."

"Why would I be disappointed? What are you talking about?"

He didn't say more, and as I brushed the sand off my feet, I realized it wasn't a coincidence that all the greatest artists in the world were celibates. I wasn't going to let him discard me; I was going to be the one doing that, not him. Dmitri's ocean had gotten into my bones, and I had to take it out, but I didn't know how.

That night, we went to the Ensenada Circus. Glittering colors fluttered on a stray dog's skirts, the outfits of the acrobats were shabby and old, and everybody waited for the big star: a boxing kangaroo. But when it appeared, it was so skinny that it couldn't box a dwarf. I couldn't stop looking at Dmitri, who was laughing like a child, while I felt barer than a late autumn tree.

Then, a team of dwarfs played games with aged monkeys and, in the middle of the show, a dwarf clown with bad makeup marched around with a banner that had a joke written on it. I laughed out loud. Dmitri didn't.

"I can't read that sign," he said.

"Is it too far for you? You probably need glasses."

"No. I'll never be able to . . . I can't."

My smile vanished. Neither of us said a word for a while. But then I couldn't stop myself.

"Is what I think true?

"Yes. I don't know how to . . ."

"But I saw you reading magazines."

"I only look at the pictures. I never had time to learn."

"Are you illiterate, then?"

"I never said I could read."

My smile faded. Giraffes went by, monkeys, dogs. Not even a small grin.

We walked out, serious, and only at the end of the street did I realized that this time he hadn't been lying. Walking back to his boat, we took the Avenida Principal, which runs parallel to the coast. The sea was sad, and the foam of the waves was more ashen than ever. He had a look of ignorance, and the wide-open eyes that come with it.

I held a stick into the water. As it entered the water, it bent. Objects seen under the water's surface are not where the eyes believe they are, I thought. I don't like water. Nothing is as it seems.

He started walking again, looking down and kicking up dust with his shoes.

"That means it's true?" I protested. He remained silent. "Answer me. I don't believe you, but answer me. Is it true?"

"Well, yes. I don't know how to read very much."

Inside me, a big wave spun everything, and I focused on the shore, noticing that a storm had made the sand confusingly muddy. He smiled, but not happily. I wanted to stop walking; he wanted to go on.

"You lied to me. Every time I gave you things to read . . . you told me you liked what I . . . everything you said . . . You're a liar . . . I knew it. Whenever I see charm I know there's dishonesty."

"I didn't lie. I didn't tell you that . . . but I didn't lie," Dmitri said, not even glancing at my eyes. I kept my eyes on his, frowning. We stayed silent, kept on walking. Sometimes silence is worse than the harshest words.

And then I realized his lie could be good for me after all. It could be my way out.

"I'm a writer, you know. I am what I write. If you can't read, you will never, ever understand me."

"I don't need to understand you to be with you."

"You will never understand the way I see things."

"You can explain to me the way you see things."

"All that business of pretending to be reading, moving your eyes from side to side. Once in a while you even stopped to frown, looking at the words."

"I was just trying to be who you wanted me to be. But I realized that no matter what I did, I'd never make you happy."

Speechless, I rocked on my legs.

He said, "I lie sometimes, but I could love you in time, you know."

What time? *I don't need him,* I thought. I only had to finish my screenplay and I could do that by myself.

I hated the word love. Such a corny word, a cliché. It's so overused that I couldn't pronounce it without curling my toes. "I don't want to be loved. I want to be respected."

"You're a coward."

"What's that supposed to mean?"

"I mean, why don't you tell me what you really feel? Why don't you tell me all the bad things you're thinking about me?" he said, jumping onto the pier. He turned around and stared at me, so I stared back. He grabbed my arm and squeezed it. Then I pulled it back and angrily pushed his chest.

"I don't want you to love me. Not you, not anyone."

"You're a bitch."

"We *artistes* have to be bitches."

I started walking ahead of him, telling myself I was going to be all right without him. He wasn't the Dmitri I believed he was anyway. I had written him without fear, without vulgarity, without lies. He was a person who could read my work and feel the same way I did. My character wasn't a fake; the real Dmitri was a fake.

"You aren't like the character in my book. He's not afraid. He never lies."

"Don't you like the real me even a little bit?'

I walked faster, and he stepped in front of me. "I don't understand you, Carla. I know you like me."

"Liking isn't enough."

"Don't you love me?"

"Love you? Hardly. On the contrary." I was saying it to convince him, but also to convince myself. We arrived at the boat, and I took three long steps toward the hatch like a Hollywood actress, grabbed my bag, and turned back.

He just looked at me and said, "Forgive me for not being who you wanted me to be."

I stepped off the boat and walked down the pier. The clouds above were pearl, pale gray, white. I didn't look back to check if he was staring at me, afraid he wouldn't be.

When I was one block away, I remembered I had forgotten to ask him for my watch back. So I headed toward the boat again; I wasn't going to talk to him or forget him; I wasn't going to kiss him or anything; I just wanted my watch back. As I walked back, I thought about what Dmitri had said a couple of days before, about icebergs and how salt is trapped beneath layers of ice. Nothing is trapped beneath my icy chest, I thought. After a few steps, I changed course and walked in the other direction, to the bus station.

I left the boat. I left Ensenada. I left him. The bus drove and I never looked back. Ahead, black soil, slate green bushes, forest green bushes, charcoal road. I counted 130 blacks and 52 greens. I didn't cry. I didn't get nervous. I didn't get upset. I didn't see him any more. I couldn't stop my legs from shaking and couldn't forget him.

I started my new life. Loneliness was nothing new for me.

Rotten Cream

A group of stubborn mules climbs the mountain wrinkles. A bitter crack in the earth bothers me. I don't like divided things.

The smell of greasy food mixes with the thick smell of gas. While I wait inside the hearse at the gas station, I turn up the volume on the radio to hear a classical duet. A group of tall Americans with hateful blue caps fixes a red truck. At the other end of the gas station, two short Americans who have broad smiles inflate the tires of an old Citröen. They all have shiny, sweaty faces and seem too happy to be real. Why does everybody have to move in groups and pairs? I travel with the kid because he fixed my car, but we are totally separate entities. His company doesn't affect my personality or decisions in any way. I know what I have to do. Go east. Finish with Dmitri.

Two American cops are staring in this direction, and I know it's not a coincidence. Maybe they're looking to challenge me to a duel; or maybe this horrible dress I'm wearing is too tight for my age, maybe I bought it under the kid's influence. The kid is taking his time in the bathroom. Hell, I told him to rush. A couple of dogs howl for food in unison. Why do they have to howl together? Can't one of them shut up? I like to do things alone. I wonder what the kid thinks about this.

I put my hands on my lap and look out through the window of the hearse at a couple of fat Americans laughing and a guy sleeping on the floor by the cash register. I start to feel a need to tell the kid . . . No, it's not a necessity . . . I just occasionally wish the kid were around, so I could share my comments with him.

No shade. No shelter. Twenty minutes is way too much time to spend in the bathroom. I'm going to pull him out of there. So I pull the car around, parking on the side by the air hose, and step out, as my left knee makes strange noises.

I try to hold on to the door of the men's room, but can't. I can't stand on my feet very long because they hurt, so I lean on the coke machine. "C'mon, kid, can we leave?"

No answer from the other side. Then the door opens and an unshaven, cross-eyed drunk smiles at me. Get out, you dirty son-of-a-bitch, I want to say, but I smile back instead.

He gestures with his head to the bathroom. "Do you want a ride, Baby?" he mumbles and spits.

"Be careful how you speak to a lady, young man!"

He smiles, his teeth yellow as rotten cream. Not in a million years. "Let's go in, there's no one inside." He raises his arm toward my face. "You still can ride, can't you?"

The cross-eyed man brings his hand to my mouth. His fingers touch my lips briefly, and I bite him. I bite him so hard he'll never forget. He squeals like a baby pig. Shoving him away, I enter the bathroom, close the door behind me, and lock it from inside.

Leaning on the door, I hear him swearing on the other side. *"You old bitch."*

My breath is fast, so I splash some water on my face. I hear the guy's footsteps walking away.

"Help!" It is the voice of the kid . . . "Help, help!" from behind one of the toilet stalls. I run and open it. The kid is lying on the floor, clutching his stomach.

"Oh, God, kid, did he hit you?"

"Who? No one hit me. I ate something that was bad, maybe the lemon candies I picked out of the trash. I think I'm dying."

This definitely can't be happening now. I don't have time for this. "Okay, kid, let's get in the car."

"I can't."

"Well, you will." Worried, I hold him, trying to pull him up, but my arms are not what they used to be, so he falls. My bones are toothpicks.

"Leave me here," the kid pushes me away. "Someone will help me. You are in a hurry. I don't want you . . . I don't want you to hate me like you hate everyone else. You hate me now, don't you?"

"C'mon. I don't hate everything. Most things, but not all."

I open the door of the bathroom and start yelling in all the languages I know, "Help, *socorro, ayuda,* Help, help!"

The group of tall guys with the truck and the cop come to help us. For a second, my mind goes blank, and I don't re-member where we are going . . . until I see the hearse. They lift up the kid and put him in the back of the hearse as if it were a bed. The kid stretches out comfortably, and one of them covers him with a blanket. I ask them for directions to a hospital, and they point to the west—the opposite direction from Dmitri. I look east. Then west. East. The kid's sick, yellowy eyes follow my disturbed gaze. If I've waited forty-nine years to see Dmitri, I can wait an hour more.

I grab the steering wheel, make U-turn and drive west. This is the first good thing I've done in my life. I hope this gives me karma points. Or at least I hope this will do when I get to purgatory.

It feels strange to help somebody. I catch myself in the rearview mirror, smiling. I don't know why I'm saving him, maybe I'm trying to save myself.

I stretch my neck and glance at him in the mirror. "You're not going to . . . how do you say it . . . die, kid. You're going to feel just fine very soon. Do you believe me?"

"I know you're lying to make me feel better, but I believe you." He pulls up his blanket and manages a smile. I turn around and wink at him through the back window. He takes his small fingers from under the blanket and waves at me.

Salmon

At the end of the road, a pale pink light rises ahead of the sun. As I glance at the kid through the rear view mirror, I notice he has fallen asleep on the beige seat of the hearse covered by a violet-blue body bag.

I decide to talk to him. Even if he's asleep, some part of his subconscious will listen anyway. And I have to tell someone. My history can't die with me.

"Since the last day I saw Dmitri until now, time has stopped. Between 1953 and now, a lot of things have happened that changed the course of history: color TV, then cable TV, then satellite TV. Nothing changed for me."

I grasp the wheel tightly, trying to find strength in it.

"I eventually moved to a salmon pink house in Ensenada, living off a job at a local radio station. With the years, my house became colder than usual, older, more solitary. On the old, bare, pale peach walls, I had faded black-and-white pictures of my dead family. I never rearranged the chocolate brown furniture. In fact, I never changed my schedule, either—I bought plain bread at the corner, ironed the wrinkles out of the sheets, and cleaned the already clean furniture over and over for years. I never understood where all the dust came from or why dust was following me."

The kid wakes up, looking at me with half-open eyes. I shut up to see if he is paying attention. With a gesture he encourages me to continue, but just then, we arrive at the hospital.

Two nurses take the kid from the back of the hearse on a gurney, pushing it to the emergency room door. The kid looks like he is in pain, yet he smiles at me.

"What happened then?" the kid asks. "You never wanted to see him again?"

"Try to relax now, kid. I'll tell you later."

"Tell me now. It distracts me from the pain."

"Well, I didn't exactly stop thinking about . . . Ninety percent of my thoughts were the same every day. I thought about death 224 times a day. One day I counted them. How I would die, blood, not blood, what would I say when I died, just normal thoughts about death like that. The other eighty-five percent of my thoughts were about the time I spent with Dmitri. I recalled each one of those days over and over. I re-remembered the events differently, depending on my mood. With the years, the memories changed so many times . . . I bought several antique daily planners for 1953 to write down the activities of each day I had spent with him, but then I kept losing the planners. It was like living in a labyrinth. That means I'm not sure which part of what I told you is what really happened, but at least I told you, because although I thought about him all the time, I never told anyone he ever existed until now."

"Why not?"

I frantically caress his forehead.

"Because I got . . . how would I put it . . . pregnant by him. An abortion was performed immediately. Of course, nothing unusual, just a complication, nothing dramatic; doctor said I wouldn't be able to have kids, that's all. So I was glad I didn't need to see Dmitri again, but I still loved the sucker. In the beginning, I counted the days that passed since the last day I saw him, the months, the years; then I surrendered counting. Every day after work, I walked to the harbor and waited by the wharf, in case he came back. Later I spent whole evenings sitting at the Victorian window, waiting for someone to show up on the corner, and watching what seemed like the same night arrive over and over. After it got dark, I walked to my caged room, to the empty kitchen, to the huge dining room. But he never . . ."

The doctor checks the kid's blood. From the doctor's expression, the kid is not all right. "Your stomach is complaining," he says. "You have to stay with us overnight. You can pick him up tomorrow, Ma'am."

He gestures to the nurses and they begin pushing his stretcher, but the kid stops them.

"What happened to the screenplay?"

"I'm not a writer, kid. Just a bitter, grouchy person carrying a notebook full of scribbles. Words that nobody reads."

The kid rubs his eyes and then holds his stomach.

"C'mon, we have to take the kid in, lady."

"Why don't you take a hike? Can't you guys see we're having a conversation here?"

I push the doctor, but the nurse passes me by, pushing the stretcher. As I see the kid being taken away, he yells to me, "Don't be scared. You'll find him."

"I'm not scared. I just don't like the idea that time is not mine. It's just that . . . Well, maybe I am a bit scared."

Behind the tinted-glass hospital door, the kid dissipates

like smoke.

I get into the hearse and look blankly at the empty passenger seat. Shiny particles gleam in the asphalt, and I know they will keep on shining although I will pass them; like the kid, those little things will keep on sparkling even when I can't watch them any more.

Old Pink

In front of the stone retirement home, there is an old American flag. Blue, red, faded red, shabby patriotic colors like my old pink dress.

Damn. My sandals let my bunions show. I put my hair up on top of my head with black stinky hair spray to cover the gray. Maybe it looks old-fashioned, but I want to look pretty. I don't really care if it looks good to him, I just need a change. I've been wearing the same face for almost seventy years.

Scared and anxious, I enter the cold building and stroll down the hall. Elderly men in robes argue about their last bowling game; elderly women in antique dresses compete for how many times a week their sons visit them.

At an aged, wooden desk, a receptionist cuts her cuticles.

"I'm looking for a . . . patient." I approach her.

"What's his last name?"

"His name is Dmitri."

"What's the patient's last name?" she asks.

"I don't know," I freeze. "I never knew." I scan her list of names.

"Never heard the name. No idea. You can check outside if you want, but I can't guarantee you'll find him," she says, pointing to the garden and returning her attention to her fingers.

As I walk through the long, windowed corridor, I check outside through the glass. The sun is high and makes me squint. As I advance to nowhere, some elderly men greet me as if they know me. They all look the same—same height, white hair. Although Dmitri might have these features now, I'm sure none of them is he. Would I be able to recognize him?

This nursing home smells of recent death and sickness. Hoping not to smell like death myself, I put some perfume on my wrists. It lasts longer there than on the neck. It has to last.

A skinny-to-the-bone, wrinkled woman grabs my arm.

"Get out of my way," I shove her hand and I am ready to run away from this ancient, crazy place, when I turn around and see a strange man at the end of the garden through the window. While all the others play in the sun, he is sitting in a wheelchair in the shade of a tree. Hanging to one side, his wrinkled hand has long fingers that hold a watch.

Quickly I swing open the door and walk toward him into the garden. As I approach, the shadows beneath the tree change position, letting me see him. His face is longer than when I met him, his skin whiter, as if his features had been contaminated by America. His hair is still curly and long, but white; his back is curved like a rock, his face as wrinkled as a dry riverbed, and his mouth open as if he were hypnotized by the wind.

From his full pocket, several watches are sticking out. Then I am sure it is Dmitri.

As I get closer, I arrange my hair. What's he going to think about me? What am I going to think about him? Forty-nine years is a long time. Really, really long.

He turns his face and sees me walking toward him. At first he doesn't recognize me. His eyebrows move. Maybe he recognizes my face, but I think he's not sure—I've certainly changed. Then he smiles, showing his gums. He has no teeth. "Hello," I say, but I'm not sure he hears me. He gazes straight at me, silent. I still don't know if he knows who I am. I can hardly walk; my legs are stiff but shaking, and my heart shivers. I lower my eyes, looking at some violets along the path and then at the blue veins in my arms. I'm not a kid anymore, either.

"Dmitri . . . ?"

"Ahhhh . . . There's only one person who calls me that . . ."

"It's me, Carla." I mumble, meaning for my voice to be loud, but it comes out a whisper.

"Carla . . ." he repeats. He widens his eyes and searches in my wrinkled face for my eyes. When he recognizes me, he sinks in his wheelchair, almost giggling lowly and faintly.

"I came to see you because I was just . . . you know . . . well, because . . ." I stumble awkwardly.

"You should have come earlier, I don't have any teeth left," he smiles with his lips shut.

"I never liked your smile anyway . . ."

We both grin with our mouths tight.

"And your hair isn't blond anymore either," I add.

"It never was blond."

I stare at him. "C'mon. Stop lying."

"My hair was brown. Remember?"

"Of course I remember. I remember everything. What do you think?"

We remain silent, listening to the movement of the tree above us in the wind.

His lips are so thin they almost disappear; he has blotches all over his skin, and his eyes are almost completely covered by his heavy eyelids, but they are still his eyes. His oceanic, grayish-blue eyes. His deep, ice cube eyes. Although they are more wisely vitreous. I don't know what to say, he doesn't help me start a conversation. He looks into my eyes. We glance down at each other's decrepit bodies and laugh. We laugh out loud, and it feels like we've been laughing like this for years.

"So what have you been doing all these years?" I ask him.

"Nothing," he shrugs. "I just stayed here."

"Of course, you found your hour-glass clock and stayed like you told me you would."

"I've found several hour-glass clocks by now. I bought them, and then I broke them all."

"Why?"

"It was fun to take the sand out."

I'm kind of disappointed by his answer. "I thought you would have traveled all over the globe."

"I think you've confused me with someone else. The only time I left the States was to cross the border with you. Never before. Never again."

"I stayed in Mexico. When I was young someone told me that 'Mexico is so far away from God and so close to the United States,'" I laugh.

"The Mexican president said that; I told you that quote."

"No, you didn't."

"Yes, I did. And you answered that you hated God."

"I've never said that," I grumble. I know I had said so, but I'd never admit it to him.

As I talk, I stare at my shoes. I can't look him in the eyes. His eyes hurt. I feel my hands shaking and sweating, and I hope he doesn't notice.

"You were surprised that I knew a quote," he mumbles.

"I must have been easily impressed back then . . ." I say, my mouth dry, my hands twisting the folds of my dress.

"No. You were curious. Always overanalyzing things, always obsessively carrying your little notebook. I liked that," he laughs, and I echo him.

"You used to tell me that you didn't like it. That I should have listened more. And I think you were right."

"But I didn't say that."

I wonder if he is right. Often memory creates what isn't there. We had a time of closeness that was left incomplete, and my imagination filled in the blanks.

"Dmitri . . . ?"

"You were always determined to call me that. I know it's probably a good Russian name for a Cold War story. But I told you many, many times, my name is Joe. You know what? It doesn't matter now, call me what you like."

"Dmitri?"

"Yes, Carla?"

"Are you still mad at me because I was mean to you?"

"Don't ask me that."

"I need to know, Dmitri."

"Why now?"

"I need to know."

"I was never mad at you. I can't be."

"I was mad at you because you killed my father."

"Killed *who?* I wouldn't kill a fly."

Surprise overtakes me. He grins. My fingers tap nervously on the wheelchair arms.

"But of course you didn't kill him. I'm just tired. I don't know what I'm saying."

Death: the word never echoes in my mind. I've lost all those years. I was dead all along. Now I have only days. I feel as if I'm in an airless, lifelong tunnel. I feel the fear of dying under my ribs.

"Are you afraid of dying now that you're close to it?" I ask him.

"I always was."

"I thought you weren't afraid of anything."

"You're so funny. You always got me confused with someone else. Maybe the guy in your book."

His fears are greater than mine. He is not the character in my screenplay. He is just a man. The only man I ever paid attention to, in order to transform him into somebody else. I have become the other him—the him I invented.

He laughs louder and I follow. I am nineteen again. I feel a fear of the immediate future. Fear of the possibly wrong next words I'm going to say, the words I didn't say, and the ones I won't say. I'm tired of the fear. I want to kiss him, at least on his cheek, at least once. I want to hear what he did with his life, even if it's boring. I look at my spotted, wrinkled hands.

"I have a lot of things to tell you," I mumble.

"Okay."

"Dmitri?"

"Yes, Carla?"

I watch some leaves tumble in the wind.

"Yes, Carla?" he asks and then begins to cough, a little at first and then more. A redheaded nurse speeds through the garden to rescue him.

I want to talk about the last day we saw each other, to say I'm sorry, but talking about that day would ruin everything. The nurse injects some clear liquid into him.

"It's time to go to sleep, Mister," she says, and then she tells me, "visiting time is over, Ma' am."

"Miss." I glance at Dmitri. He looks at my empty ring finger. Now he knows I never married.

Dmitri coughs again, more violently. The nurse raises his arms, but she can't stop the cough. I fake coughing a little on purpose, in order to accompany him. We make a duet of coughs.

"What time is it in Egypt now?" I ask him out of the blue, and he gapes at me surprised. He has to concentrate on my question and stops coughing. With his hands shaking, he pulls a few watches out of his pocket. He picks a small stainless steel watch from the pile. "It's 11 P.M. in Cairo, eleven and two minutes," he says, and coughs lightly twice to recompose himself.

The nurse stares at the watches and her face turns as red as her hair. "Hey, you bastard, that's my watch there!" She grabs her fluorescent yellow Swatch and puts it on, cursing. Then she starts to push the wheelchair, taking him away.

"Dmitri! Why?"

He stops the wheels of his chair. "Why what?"

"Why did you steal my watch? What was the story?"

He laughs. "Story. What story? I wasn't the one inventing watch stories. That was you. To put them in your script. Don't you remember?"

I look at his watches; the various metals shine mischievously, changing colors. "Why did you like me then?"

"I don't know. You had a sad beauty somehow."

I wrote that forty-nine years ago—a sad beauty. He couldn't know it. He couldn't read my notebook.

The nurse stares at us, without understanding.

"How did you know I wrote that?"

"I didn't. Couldn't you tell things about me I never said?"

"Maybe . . ."

The nurse takes him away from me. "Bye . . ." I mumble.

"Let's not say good-byes. We'll talk tomorrow," Dmitri says, tapping his chest. "We have every day free now."

While I watch the nurse disappear with the wheelchair into the home, for a moment I think he is right, that I am free because I have already paid the price of being mean to him with all of my loneliness.

I take a small mirror from my purse and look at my eyes—they are not two round circles anymore, but two lines. I'm not so sure if I feel free. All my life I missed living by living in his imaginary life. All these years waiting to see him and for what?

I walk out of the retirement home, wheezing, out of breath and see thin, bare yellow trees stuck there, all the same, boring size. My legs tremble like feathers in the wind. I'm not going to be able to drive, so I head to the taxi stand. A taxi driver, who has a small TV playing a western, waits for fares in the front of the retirement home. "Only a few people get out of here alive, Ma'am."

I wonder if I'm alive, just because I'm free to go out on the streets. No, I'm trapped like the moon in the night. I think I won't be free while Dmitri lives.

Taxi Yellow

I've told the taxi driver to drive in circles because I'm not sure where I want to go yet. I'm used to circles, labyrinths.

On the radio, I hear that American women dislike wearing yellow even more than orange or brown. They're wrong. Orange is a hateful color. Although this anger eats me up, hatred made me write:

> The other Cartier diamond watch was from a queen who had a collection of shoes, but had never seen the ocean because she was afraid of water. She just couldn't allow herself to stop being a queen long enough to see reality. I haven't found my favorite watch yet, though. I travel all around the world and can't find it. I want an hour-glass clock, so I can control time. I could turn it whenever I want the sand to move, and I could stop time whenever I want.

I was never writing about Dmitri—there's no such thing as objectivity. I was the one who wanted to escape from my family, the one who hated my father, the one who never saw the ocean, not even when it was in front of me. I was the one who would have liked to have had an hour-glass clock to control things. Control feelings. Control fears. Control time. Time cheated me.

The words accumulated in my notebook, until I finally filled it and had a shadow of a screenplay. A great shadow, but never a script.

I never finished anything in my life, but I will tomorrow. The real Dmitri has to die, so my creation will survive. He has to die, so no one realizes I lied about him, that he is not the real him I saw.

━━━━━

Truth hits us over and over, like waves pounding the shore; but also like the tide, sometimes it arrives gently.

It's 3 A.M. in this cheap hospital room where the kid is. He dreams in his bed; I lie on the uncushioned cot beside him, feeling a slight oppression in my chest, a weary grief inside me. I haven't been able to sleep because memories have come and gone all night. I wish I could recover from my past, like the kid from his stomachache.

The only way to escape an awful reality is in the mind. The stories I made up were what kept me alive all those years. I clenched my fists around an imaginary past to win days in a poker game against death. But does Dmitri deserve to die just because he thawed me? I glance at the gun under my pillow—its shape is elegant, its color cold. I'm scared to lose him again and scared to die before him.

"Are you okay?" the kid asks half asleep, "You look kind of worried."

"Me? I've never been better," I roll over, feeling the gun's steel gray coldness on my ear and tasting murder in my mouth.

Filled with a sudden happiness, I try to stand up, but my weak knees don't obey, and I fall to the floor, face down.

"Kid, I can't move my . . ."

"Nurse!"

"Don't call the nurse. Help me. Let's get out of here.

My shaky hands hold my thighs. My legs don't move. Won't move. Can't move.

Khaki

First I look at my brown shoes on the wheelchair the kid stole from the hospital, and then up at the American flag in the front of the retirement home. Just because my legs won't work doesn't mean my mind will stop racing. Everything is going to be fine. Just fine, I repeat to myself, caressing my pocket, touching the outline of the sweet gun.

I don't know if I'm going to kill him right away. The afternoon has more appropriate colors for dying. Besides, I want to ask him more questions, like if he thought of me all those years. So I slip my right hand inside my pocket and tighten my fingers on the gun, just to feel its buried coldness.

Looking as calm as ever, I wheel in, smiling through the corridors toward his room, aware of the sound of my own breathing.

I have a fried-yellowtail sandwich in a cardboard box, and I know he'll be happy I brought his favorite food. I hope his tastes haven't changed with time. "There's always a sandwich that someone left somewhere. It's just a question of finding it," Dmitri used to say. He didn't want to be rich; he actually chose to be poor. Not all men want the same things, I guess. I turn right into another corridor. Not all people escape in the same way. I escaped within myself.

As soon as I arrive at the room that has his name on the tag, I peer around the door—the room is clean, his bed empty. Clean. Empty. White. He has disappeared again.

Static, I stay there in my wheelchair, leaning on the door,

supporting myself on the doorknob. On one of his shelves, I see a broken hour-glass clock. The clock is an antique piece made of dark wood with simple, silver detailing. The khaki sand is not running; it fell a long time ago.

"He's gone," a nurse behind me says.

"I can see that. Where did he go?"

"I'm sorry, Ma'am."

I lower my eyes, staring at the flimsy cardboard box in my left hand. I hold it tighter than ever. I wonder if I should throw it away. I don't know what to do.

"What?"

"He passed away."

"No. It can't . . . but we have to talk today, you know, talk. I have to ask him if . . . I have to get my watch back. I have to . . . have to see . . ."

"I understand," the nurse says and coughs, but she doesn't understand a damned thing.

"I forgot to . . . I forgot to tell him I loved . . ."

My hands shake totally out of control like in Nirvana. My breath is cut short and I open my nostrils wide, as if wanting to breathe the world, swallowing my words for a second. A painful hole stings in my chest and spreads its confused sadness to my bones.

"What happened?" I mumble.

"We don't know yet. He laughed like crazy all night by himself. God knows what he was remembering. And when I found him dead this morning, he had his eyes open wider than ever and a smile on his face," the nurse scratches her nose. "Sometimes elderly people just choke from laughing too much. Or maybe he had a heart attack because he was so happy. In short, he died of laughter."

"He died of laughter?"

"He wrote a note before he died. Do you want to read it?" She takes a piece of paper out of her pocket.

"That's impossible," I say. "He was illiterate."

"He'd been trying to learn how to read and write this last year. He told me he had to read a screenplay based on him; he even made me look for a writer. Italian last name. Some woman. Her name was something like Caroline, but I never found anything by her. I guess he was delirious. I still think it's great that he was trying to learn to read at his age." The nurse smiles at me, and I answer with a harsh look.

She winces and looks at the paper. "Are you the wife?"

Without hesitation, I nod.

"Here. I guess you can have it." She hands me the paper and walks away, and the sound of her white heels taps down the corridor. The sound fades, leaving only my heartbeat.

I unfold the paper. It says in the firm compressed writing of a child: *I don't know what time it is in North Korea now Thanks for stopping by.*

Frozen here in this awful, pale pink corridor with the sandwich box in my hands, I taste irony and leave the box on a bench. Maybe someone will pick it up. Death won this hand, but maybe he did love me . . . Otherwise, why was he looking for my screenplay?

I keep the note in my hands awhile and lift up my face. I want to count colors. Can't. Don't see any. Everythingseems black-and-white. Want to scream. Tell everybody our story.

How we met when he stole my watch, and how he used to compare everything to oceans, and how much he liked boats and sails and the sky and clouds and wind. How much I liked him. How much maybe I loved him.

I hated him because it was easier than forgetting him. He was a scab in my memory I just couldn't pick. My fists are tight, lips tight, and I press them tighter, without worrying about the wrinkles anymore. Swallowing my heavy saliva, slouching, I wheel myself in no particular direction. I feel the gun now heavier in my pocket.

Mustardy Yellow

This morning, at the wake, I wheeled around in my chair passing people, sad people, tired people, weeping people, people crying, yelling, sobbing, friends, family. A black mass of unfamiliar faces.

There were flowers and statues of virgins and death symbols. There were musicians and kids running. There was a smell of rush and reed. There was a long corridor with lilac fluorescent light and a butter yellow room at the end.

Dmitri's son, the priest, played with five poor boys from the church. They hugged him and laughed.

Advancing down the corridor, I met the widow again and noticed a look of jealousy in her eyes. She shouldn't have felt jealous; she was the real widow; I lost him almost fifty years ago. Suspecting she might kill me right there at the wake, I scowled; my eyes fixed on her chubby face. She smiled kindly with compassion. She was not hunting me; I've been hunting myself, always have. I alone hunted my feelings to kill them. I grabbed them, suffocated them, buried them inside me. I chewed my heart and learned to live without one for forty-nine years and 241 days.

I waited in line to pay my last respects to the corpse. A long and slow file to give the last farewell.

The dead body was wearing a cheap, brown suit. I moved forward to the coffin and touched his forehead with my fingertips to check if it really was cold like the books said. His skin was as cold as a patio tile in winter. His face was not pale white or gray, as I imagined it would be, but mustardy yellow. His dead skin had blue spots, blue like ripe plums. His eyes, faded ice-cube-colored then, were open. I didn't close them. Instead, I leaned forward above the coffin, wondering if he would see me.

In silence, I told him, "Forgive me for everything I didn't do." My heart raced as if chasing a bird inside my chest, wishing he would answer.

After I leaned for a long time above his face, people in line behind me eventually nudged my wheelchair to the side. But I stayed in a dark corner until the last person left the wake, until I watched the lid of the coffin close on his face. I was the only one left when they did it. The only one who saw it. The only one who needed to see it to make sure he was gone.

In the distance, all the white tombstones on the green slopes look the same. I'm alone at the cemetery. Because of the heavy rain, nobody came. Only a crazy person would come to a rainy burial. I don't know how I can still be in this cemetery, focusing on the hole prepared for his coffin. The memory of the sound of the spade digging in and out of the dirt mound echoes in my head, mingling with the present sound of the rain tapping my hat, the sound of sadness. I will not cry.

My dress is stuck to my skinny body, my shoes soaked, my feet cold, my hair is all over my face, my face has no expression at all. The grass has that nice, wet smell. I watch the rain fall, the soil forming muddy clods on the coffin, the water wrestling with the mud, washing the coffin in brown.

For a moment, I wonder what I'm going to do after the funeral. What am I going to do tomorrow? And the day after tomorrow? Who's going to be standing here when they bury me? I'm like a puzzle with missing pieces. I had all the pieces once.

I was so afraid of making the wrong move that I didn't make any. I don't move now. I'm sitting here in the rain, staring at the mud falling into the hole. The coffin is a vague shape down there. I don't even move my eyelashes.

The flowers are down there in the hole. Why are violets called violets if they are blue? Why are some roses yellow? Who the hell gave them these names? I count the flowers. Ten, eleven, twelve, maybe eleven, but because it's raining, I can't count them right. I have water in my eyes.

Maybe I'm weeping a little. Maybe it's not me who is crying. Maybe it's some other woman. I don't know if she's crying for him or for me.

Black coffin; black mud; wet, black shoes.

It feels nice to cry when it rains, it's like crying with someone else.

Dirty Beige

The old Pueblo de Los Angeles near Union Station is dirty beige. A place where the people of the First and Third worlds collapse, buying and selling regional food and crafts. All the people are sepia, like a faded, old picture. The dust in the air is also beige; I can even taste dirt on my cracked lips.

As the floor spins a little, people are blurred and stretched. I carry the gun in my pocket just in case someone hates me before I can hate them. One good thing about Mexicans is that they'll never kill for no reason like Americans sometimes do. Latinos have to have a reason to kill. I wonder if I have one.

I wheel around, facing south. Wheeze out of breath. Take five painkillers. Then another one. Three guys run, crossing Olvera Street; one of them carries a basket with roosters for a fight—some of them are gray and white, the others are the awful, uncountable color orange. They have that color on purpose to bother me. Their only purpose at this moment is to cross the street to fight to kill, to survive. If I cross or don't cross, it is the same. As I observe the green light changing to red, I try to find something, some reason to cross.

People freeze on the corner, so I freeze, too. Something must have happened, something I don't know. I hate waiting. And they know it. I'm in a perfect situation to kill. Not because I have a gun, but because I don't have anything to lose that was not already lost.

More and more people begin to surround me, waiting for

the light to change. They watch me. There is nothing new about that. They want to contaminate me. They want me to have feelings like theirs. I grab the gun inside my pocket, turn my eyes around, and easily spot an elderly Latino couple who deserve to die. He wears flat, orange sneakers. Anyone who wears orange deserves to die. And anyone who goes out with someone who wears orange.

When the light changes, I advance toward them. The noise of the city echoes in my head: echoing horns, random chattering, people swearing in Spanish. I glance around to check if anyone is looking at me. The colors people wear are turquoise, bright red, bright green, fluorescent yellow. No one can see me in this mess.

I lose sight of the couple in the crowd for a second. A frustrated feeling of bitterness fills my pupils. Then I spot them again. The Latino woman has long white hair and a big frown on her thick lips. As I move closer I hear her tell him what he should do, and he tells her he won't do it. I hold my gun. With my thumb, I pet the trigger, speculating about what her last words would be if I killed her. I bet she would curse me. So I grab the gun with all my fingers and tighten my grip. Maybe she'll say one word, like "killer," or "no." Just one word. Maybe none. Maybe she will just look at him and won't need to say anything. I'm not very far away; I can shoot her white hair from here and make it turn red.

What would I do after I fire? They'd probably catch me very easily. In the States, if you kill someone, you are innocent until proven guilty. In Mexico, you are guilty until you prove the contrary. In the U.S., you go to jail right away.

I could keep dying in jail. The only difference would be the sun, which is too orange for me anyway. The couple keeps arguing while they turn the corner, and I get the feeling that even if they argue they'll never be apart. I wasn't abandoned by Dmitri. I chose to abandon him.

A fear worse than hatred shakes my body, so I slow down, letting the elderly couple go. I don't hate them enough to kill them. Probably they don't hate orange. Probably they don't hate me. Perhaps they don't hate at all. I look around to see if someone noticed I was going to kill them. No one is following me. No one hates me enough to kill me either. No one sees me. I'm invisible. Maybe no one ever saw me.

I have rehearsed my final words many times like a speech. As the years passed, I changed my last words as many times as seasons changed. But the only person I ever cared for left without saying anything. Now, I don't have anyone to say good-bye to. No one to hate that much to keep on living.

I don't want to let destiny decide when I have to die. I won't let time control me. I caress my gun. How many years would they give me for killing time? I sink my finger into the left side of my chest, trying to feel how deep my end could be.

Christmas Green and Red

The kid is playing with the cards by himself on his hotel bed, using them as if they were cars, moving them back and forth on the thin mattress. I take a couple of painkillers to rest. I don't want to feel better, I just want to feel nothing.

Then I place my head on the hard, square pillow and stare at the pattern on the shabby, green rug, while I angrily tighten my fingers and then calmly release them. The walls are so thin here I hear people in the next room making love. Slowly I move my head toward the wall, hear muffled voices. The kid is smiling to himself. I wonder what would have happened if I'd married and had kids.

"Well, I always knew I was never going to get married," I grumble almost to myself.

"How can you be so sure you won't get married some time?" the kid says, challenging me.

"There are some things you know when you're almost eighty."

"You can marry me if you want. I hate girls, but I like you." He stares at me.

"I don't think your mother would like me."

The kid scratches the scars on his forehead, "I don't care about her, I care about you. You don't look good. Maybe you should pray or something . . ."

"I don't pray," I growl with a rough voice. "Do you pray?"

"No, but I've seen people do it. It looks really easy."

"If it's so easy, why don't you pray?"

"I don't need to pray. I talk without speaking," he says and mixes the cards.

"With God?" I ask.

The kid smiles and shakes his head. "Yeah, and with things." Then he starts to sort the queens on the bed. "Like dogs, plants, bugs. I talk to the TV sometimes. If you like what you see, you communicate with things."

I stare at him, listening to the sound of crickets. "I know what my problem is now, kid. I don't have a reason to die. I just don't want anything any more." I squint through the window, but without really seeing. One gray, two grays, three grays.

"I want something," he mutters.

"To find your father?" I mock, trying to make him smile.

"No. I don't have a father. He's dead. I just lied to you, so you'd take me out of that horrible hospital."

"You lied to me?"

"It was a good lie."

There are no good lies or bad lies. I think about where this knowledge took me. Nowhere. I lost the only man who mattered because of my stubbornness about lies. I'm not going to let it happen again.

"You're right. It was a good lie."

"Besides, I don't need my father or my mother any more, I found you," the kid looks at me with big, bright eyes.

I look at his opened lips, knowing his games. He is waiting for me to ask him what he wants. "Okay. What do you want, kid?"

"I want a Christmas tree with red bows, green balls, and lights. I want to celebrate Christmas with you."

"But it's July!"

"You said time didn't matter."

＝＝＝

The only sound is the gutter water weaving like a snake down the street. The afternoon is quiet, maybe too quiet.

We abandon the hearse in a vacant lot. Our trip to the past is over. We are seated at a table outside a Mexican taqueria in East LA. I sit on top of my parcel of money.

"After we find a Christmas tree, we go back to Mexico, okay?"

He nods and orders a burrito, a cola, and an orange soda so he can mix both drinks in a glass to see the colors melt. I think about having a whiskey because I've run out of painkillers.

"Whiskey without ice, please," I order. "And a cheese sandwich without ham, just cheese." The waiter leaves.

"You can always tell if the cheese is rotten by the color, kid, but they can always wash the ham with soap to get its original color. As you can see, colors can save you from dying."

"Colors saved you."

"What do you mean?"

"Colors let you escape from bad memories."

I try to cleanse my heart's memory, to leave it clear as fresh water, but bad memories float up like big bubbles.

"Maybe memory doesn't exist, kid, only imagination.

Maybe memory is an illusion and remembering just a device to deny the passage of time."

"What are you saying? Don't you see that your memories have kept you alive?"

I look up, knowing he is right, and suddenly I feel my past lighter, as if it were made of butterfly wings. A girl offers me leather belts and shell necklaces. She is more or less the kid's age and has Indian red skin. She has long, brown hair with orange split ends. The color doesn't bother me as much as I thought it would.

"No," I say calmly. By the kid's red cheeks, I know he likes the girl. The Native American girl stares at him. He plays with his earring in his right ear. I lift my glass of whiskey slowly, aware that my movements are shakier now. The girl shrugs and walks away. The kid looks at her with big eyes, noticing her dull expression.

"That girl is not for you, anyway."

"Are you jealous?"

"Maybe . . . a little."

I notice the sad expression in the kid's eyes, watching the girl leave. "You don't want to like her anyway. She looks bored."

"How can she get bored? I never get bored. I always have something to look at."

I glance around and don't see anything. "What do you see?"

"I see a Volkswagen Sirocco and a beautiful girl who is leaving."

To him white is white. To him a Sirocco is a car. To me,

the sirocco is a hot wind in Italy, and when it comes, people go crazy because of it. Although any wind or anybody can make you crazy, if you want to be crazy. I guess all my life I looked for someone to blame for my craziness. I'm tired of blaming, tired of escaping.

The kid has small, dirty hands, and I imagine them becoming older and wrinkled like mine. I release my hand from the gun in my pocket, and take the yellowing pages of my screenplay from the bag. Without hesitation, I write "THE END" on the last page. I wrote the last scene after I left Dmitri. The story was not perfect or polished, but it was finished, like me, a long time ago. Then I give it to the kid with nearly three thousand dollars in twenty-dollar bills.

"Look, kid, don't misunderstand me. It's not that I learned to love you or anything, but this money is too heavy for me to carry around, so I'd rather you have it."

"We can spend the money going to nice places."

"I don't think I could spend all this money in two days— if I still have two days. And anyway, there's nothing I want."

"Are you sure?"

The kid peels the gold foil off the soda bottle, folds it, and makes two golden bands. He puts one around my ring finger and the other around his.

I smile silently, take his little hand, and kiss it. The blue sky coats the afternoon transforming it into pastel shades.

The kid clutches the bag, hugging it with one hand and holding mine with the other. I look at the street, the cars seem to move more slowly than ever.

Foggy Gray

Smell of gas, onions, wine, rotten fruit, sweat. The kid pushes my wheelchair through small stores and busy markets to find a tree. My throat is dry from the sun. At least in the car I had windows to protect me.

We try a couple of small stores, but we can't find a damned tree. No one has a Christmas tree in July.

My voice gets husky. I cough. I feel tired. Did I eat today? I think I haven't eaten for days. I can't remember how many.

With my palm, I stop the wheel of the chair at a red light, glancing around. Old, washed walls, faded graffiti. People begin to surround me, waiting for the light to change. Across the street, two policemen also wait, looking in my direction. I am obviously clenching a gun in my pocket. One of the policemen points at me. I puff. Cough. Cough again. The light changes, and I stay still, watching people rush to get to the next corner. The masses cross fast before my eyes and suddenly a gray fog starts to cover everything I see.

Damn. I must look pathetic, struggling, puffing fast, coughing and coughing. The air is kind of stuck, heavy. There is not even a drop of wind. Dust caresses my cheeks. I feel like dust, light, hazy.

The policemen run to me, reaching for their guns. I gasp. I need air. I reach for my gun and pull it out of my pocket, but my arm drops involuntarily. The kid pulls my arm to move it, but he can't move it. My finger is tightened on the trigger. A shot is heard, I think, and maybe a bullet hits the ground not far away. I feel my throat closing. It feels dry; I can't even swallow my own saliva. I try to clear my throat. I try to speak but can't. I spit, leaving a blood spot on the floor. So this is death? Am I really dying? My thin bones are tired. Everything starts to sway. I slide down the wheelchair and my knee bones make a cracking sound. I fall over backwards, reaching the ground with a dry thud on the concrete; finally I am lying down on the sidewalk, face up.

I can't move, my body is as stiff as thick cement. A chill runs all over my back. I feel the back of my head on the sidewalk. This is what the doctor told me would happen: my neck is inflamed. My bones are the bars of my prison. My body is my own jail.

This is what they told me: People don't die of leukemia, they die because there's no defense against an infection or hemorrhage. Everything begins to explode inside your body. I want to talk but can't move my jaw. My lips are heavy, numb.

Onlookers begin to gather around. Above me, I see colors . . . Deformed faces discuss what they should do. Don't you see I can't breathe? No words come out of my mouth, just a muffled shriek.

The kid yells my name, and I see his face pushing through the middle of the crowd. I slowly move my clammy fingers, but he doesn't see them. I can hear you, kid. I'm down here, under these eyes.

"It's me. The kid. Your kid. Do you remember me?"

Of course I remember, I want to say, but only a gasp comes out of my mouth. Will you remember me when I'm gone? How much time will it take for you to forget me?

It's too late to ask him. There is no time. Images of my past melt like clouds. If I die, who will remember?

The kid gives my hand little kisses. I feel sad leaving him alone, but at least he has the money. A policeman asks him for the bag but he scurries away, watching from a safe distance, sobbing as I am moved to a stretcher.

Strange faces spin as I am pushed away. My eyes want to close. My strength vanishes inside my body like snowflakes touching hot metal.

I wonder if this is what Dmitri felt when he died. No. He died of happiness; everybody knows cancer is the disease of sorrow.

I killed myself, the person I should have loved the most, before I could really love myself enough.

Orange

The ambulance speeds up, shaking over the uneven pavement. My arms and legs tremble with it. The metallic medical instruments clang. I'm not going to make it to the hospital. I'm glad. No more hospitals for me.

I have an oxygen feed in my nose and a respirator on. Can hear my smooth heartbeats on a machine somewhere behind my head. Feel my ribs expand and compress slowly, like a dog's sleeping breath.

Since I was a kid, I was ready to die, but now I'm not so sure. It's cold in here. Maybe it's the whiteness of the walls. There are no colors. Am I already dead?

I really want to sleep. The ambulance lights gleam and spin and make strange shadows on the window. In my reflection my skin looks dark yellow, my lips pale violet. Everything sounds like a pearl inside a shell, coated with deformed underwater sounds. My eyelids feel heavy. I'm afraid to close my eyes. I'm afraid that if I close them, I won't be able to open them again. Does it have to be today? I didn't do much today after all, didn't go to the pier, didn't see Dmitri, didn't hate enough, didn't cry.

Warm water fills my underwear. Finally I have lost control. Now my body is an open, empty cage. Only now, I close my eyes. My bones sink into the sheets like sugar dissolving in water. An unexpected sweat shakes me and a sweet coldness embraces me. My pupils turn up and around.

I don't have any more pain. No cough. No thought. No

hate.

Heavy lids tremble over eyes that don't see. Colors flash by like lighting in the dark. With daring calmness, I count colors in my swirling, sweet-liar memory.

Counting.

One olive black pirate-sword earring.

Counting.

Two oceanic blue-gray eyes.

Counting.

One dawn-fading red sun.

Almost orange.

Counting.

One orange.

Two orange.

Three . . .

Acknowledgments

Paul Williams, Todd A. Sharp,

Jessica Postigo, John Rechy,

Phillips Guebauer, Jonathan David,

Joan Tewkesbury, Monica Rizzo,

Sarah Luck Pearson, Jay Frasco,

Del Reisman, Lila Yacob,

Sherie Yang, Anya Booker,

Julieann Getman, Pia Celemente,

Kelly Reiter, Martin Lazarini,

Kelly Reiter, Freeman Scott,

Carlos Tobal, Dalmiro Saenz,

Jorge Lanata, Marci Abadi,

all my cousins, uncles and aunts

A Note on the Type

The text was set in 11.5 point Aldus with a leading of 15.5 points space. Hermann Zapf designed Aldus for the Stempel foundry in 1954 as a companion to his Palatino typefaces. Originally designed as a display typeface, Palatino gained popularity as a text typeface as well. Believing Palatino to be too bold for settings at small point sizes, Zapf designed the lighter weight Aldus to better suit text settings. The typeface is named for Aldus Manutius, the innovative fifteenth-century Italian printer/publisher.

━━━━━━

The display font is Futura, a compass-and-pen typeface, designed by the German book designer, Paul Renner. The Bauer Foundry released this typeface circa 1928. Single weight strokes are characteristic of Futura and the number of strokes used to create the letters are minimized. The o is a perfect circle, and the a, b, d, p, and q were designed by adding a straight line.

━━━━━━

Composed by Stephanie Frey
Allentown, Pennsylvania

Printed and bound by
Maple-Vail Book Manufacturing Group
Binghamton, New York

DATE DUE	
Jul 14, 2001	
	PRINTED IN U.S.A.